SADDLE WISE
3

SCHOOL DAY RIDES

Inda
Schaenen

RP KIDS
PHILADELPHIA · LONDON

Dedication

This story is dedicated to Emily Jolly and Jordan Leonard,
who knew April and Rainy Day from the beginning,
and graciously and energetically read these stories
with much appreciated insight.

Library of Congress Control Number: 2009922094

ISBN 978-0-7624-3360-5

Cover illustration by Robert Papp
Cover and interior design by Frances J. Soo Ping Chow
Icons illustrated by Rich Kelly
Edited by Kelli Chipponeri
Typography: Affair and Berthold Baskerville

Published by Running Press Kids,
an imprint of Running Press Book Publishers
2300 Chestnut Street
Philadelphia, PA 19103-4371

Visit us on the web!
www.runningpress.com

Chapter

Crickets make it impossible to forget that school's about to start. Just when you think you can go out for an August ride, nothing in the world but you, your horse, and the squeaks of leather and the smell of warm horsehide, those infuriating chirps swell to a fever pitch in the seedy grass along the road. It's like they're whispering right in your ear—"binders, pencils, loose-leaf paper, calculator, milk cartons, homework, grades...Hey, you in the saddle, tomorrow you gotta go back to school."

Why *are* crickets so much louder in August than June? As if sensing my distraction, Rainy Day stumbled on a loose stone on the road but regained his balance. He shook out his mane and mouthed his bit.

"Sorry, boy," I said, taking a firmer hold on the reins and returning my weight to the center of his back. I heeled his flanks and, with a snort, Rainy Day advanced into a steady trot, kicking up a low dusty cloud behind us. We weren't even a mile out of town, but Plattsburgh was so small, it didn't take long to get to the country.

So much had happened since seventh grade ended, it felt like ages since I had to think about anything but horses. First, in May, there was the terrible truck accident that had nearly killed Rainy Day. A trailer transporting a load of horses to a slaughterhouse had crashed and overturned on the highway, killing many and leaving the rest of them wounded and shocked. Aunt Patti and I had been driving on the highway when it happened. We came to a halt right behind the accident site. I was standing by the side of the road when a bleeding Rainy Day appeared behind me and nudged my shoulder. From that moment on, our lives were connected and my fears of horses and riding melted away. In the confusion that followed, Rainy Day and I found each other like a couple of wandering souls. Up until that moment, I had been deathly afraid of horses. But the accident changed everything. I guess I should say that Rainy Day changed everything. All I could think about was bringing him home to a safe place, where his wounds could heal and he could live his life in peace. So I adopted him and learned to ride, which had taken up just about all of my time from that moment until now. After that I learned to care for a foal, and helped train him while also taking care of the animals on the McCann farm.

In the last four months, I had hardly spent any time at all

with my school friends. Now I was worried about all the social reshuffling that was bound to happen in eighth grade. You never know how the cliques are going to work out until you're in the middle of a cafeteria. And even then, there's no telling what will happen from day to day. That was one thing I appreciated about spending all summer doing farm chores—it was predictable. Animals need the same thing every single day—food, water, a clean place to stay, and companionship. The whole life of a farm is built around those needs. And even when things were unpredictable—like when one of the geese got out of their pen and made it all the way to the pond—what you're supposed to do is usually obvious.

I was also concerned about how I would manage to keep up with schoolwork, be on a sports team, or do some other extracurricular activity (which at my school was mandatory), and also have enough time and energy to ride and groom Rainy Day. Even without school and a social life all summer, I found farmwork exhausting. For sure I would have to give up working at the McCann place. Luckily, Nelson McCann understood my other commitments and was thinking about hiring a replacement. But wouldn't Rainy Day get lonely all day without me? Should I think about moving him to the McCann's so he would have other horses to be with?

I was lost in my own thoughts when we got to the crest of a hill about three miles out of town. I brought Rainy Day to a halt and wheeled him around. It was a view I always liked. Below us, the Ozark hills of Missouri rolled toward the river valleys. Considering it was the end of August, the fields of soy and corn were still pretty green. That was because of the disastrous rains in May, when the ground was saturated with water, and all the small creeks and rivers overflowed their banks and flooded Plattsburgh and other towns. It seemed hard to believe what Rainy Day and I had been through together in only four months. I reached down and patted his neck.

"Well, do we keep going or turn around and go home?" I asked.

He stomped one foot and lifted his chin to point back down the hill. Evidently he was all done climbing.

"Okay." I laughed, clucking him back down the steep hill. I had to lean back in the saddle as we trotted toward home.

A few minutes later I began to hear something other than Rainy Day's heavy panting, the double beat of clip-clopping hooves, and chirping crickets. We rounded a bend and came face-to-face with a dozen boys running up the hill in the opposite direction. I knew right away it was our middle-school cross-country team, because I saw Lowell, my next door-neighbor. Lowell was one of my best friends. We had known each other ever since we were four years old. My aunt Patti used to take care of him when his parents were at work, so we pretty much grew up playing on the same swing set, digging in the same sandbox, and taking turns on the same tricycle. Lowell's face was beet red, and sweat clumped his longish blond hair into dark strings. Some of the other kids I recognized; others must have been going into seventh grade. Lowell had told me that the coach was calling practices the week before school started so kids would be ready to compete in the first meet of the season.

"Hey," I called out to Lowell, holding Rainy Day steady.

Seeing that it was me, one of the jerkier kids in our class, David Faust, elbowed Lowell in the side and said, "Hey, look who's here."

Another kid whacked Lowell on the back and said, "Dude, here's your chance to ride off into the sunset."

Lowell looked annoyed as the team ran by. Everyone knew that Lowell and I had been friends since we were practically toddlers, that his mom and my aunt Patti were friends and all, but some people just couldn't deal with it and constantly teased him about being in love with me. I turned and watched them jog away.

Lowell had gotten into running and working out at the end of seventh grade. It was like a switch had been flipped, and he just decided not to be a gloomy and bitter hermit, spending all his time gaming and watching stuff on the Internet. I had overheard Lowell's mom tell Aunt Patti how relieved she was that Lowell was finally taking school and himself seriously. "I know what you mean," Aunt Patti had replied. "Lowell's one of the brightest boys I know. It was a shame to watch him disappear."

Before running out of view, a couple of the boys spat off to the side of the road. I was happy that Lowell had finally found a sport that suited him, but I wondered about what would work for me. A couple of my friends were going to play field hockey, but I couldn't really think of an extracurricular activity I wanted to do. I told myself to quit fretting and try to enjoy the last day of vacation.

"Come on, Rainy Day," I said. "Let's really go." The road leveled off, and I nudged him into a canter. As it flattened even more, I let him go full speed into a gallop. It had taken me a long time to feel in control when we galloped, but now we knew what to expect from each other. Rainy Day wouldn't run off willy-nilly, and I would slow him down the minute I felt uncomfortable with the speed. I leaned forward against the saddle horn, watching the road ahead, and couldn't help but smile as the hot August wind rushed against my face.

After brushing and grooming Rainy Day and setting him up with fresh hay and water, I went into the house and sat on the floor of my room with the thick back-to-school envelope that had come in the mail the week before. I hadn't been ready to face what was inside—forms, rules, schedules, and sign-up sheets. But now I had no choice. Tomorrow morning at seven-thirty I had to be in my assembly seat listening to the principal give his annual pep talk. Before reading anything else, I picked up our class list, which showed the names and addresses of every single eighth grader. First I looked at mine: April Helmbach. But right above my name was one I had never seen before: Matthew Heisman, 75 Pin Oak Lane. Pin Oak Lane was in the nicest part of town, where the big old wooden houses had three stories, wraparound porches, and huge yards. There had been no Matt Heisman in seventh grade, and I couldn't think of any other kid with that last name. But because he was right next to me in alphabetical order it meant we would sit next to each other at the weekly assemblies. Within a minute I had made a picture of him in my head—cute, preppy, great smile, and clever. Maybe he was a soccer ace with a rich dad who commuted to work as a CEO in St. Louis, and his mom had a huge diamond on her ring finger. They wanted a more relaxed environment for their children and so moved to humble little Plattsburgh. Even though I had no idea whether it was true or not, the story made me excited to meet this Matt.

The only other new name on the list was Monica Shinkel. A sweet name, but I couldn't seem to make up a story about her. Nothing came to mind by way of a background for someone named Monica Shinkel. I put down the class roster and stared at the list of school supplies. Then I looked at my schedule for the first week of school. It wasn't too bad, actually. They had put me in high math, which was good. And I had a few study halls right after lunch, which was also good.

Just then my dog, Chase, pushed open the door of my room and started to walk over all the papers I had spread out on the floor on his way to greeting me.

"No, Chase, back off," I said. "Sorry, but hang on. Let me get these back into a pile."

Once everything was back in the envelope and on my

desk, I scooped Chase up onto my bed and lay down with my earphones on to listen to music. It had been the last day in a perfect summer. But nothing lasts forever. I simply had to face the fact that things were going to be different. Yes, I definitely felt some dread about going back to school, but even I had to admit that, judging by the nerves bouncing around in my stomach, I was also kind of psyched.

Chapter

2

"I wondered when you were going to show up," Aunt Patti said with a smile, getting up to kiss the top of my head the next morning at seven A.M. "Are you walking with Lowell?"

"Yeah," I said, pouring myself some cereal and ignoring Chase begging at the counter. "We're meeting at seven-twenty. I've already mucked out Rainy Day's stall and set him up to graze all day."

"Wow," Aunt Patti said. "Kind of a major start to the first day of school. Oh, listen, Nelson will be here for dinner. I hope that's okay."

"Sure, fine, whatever," I said. I was too distracted to object, not that I had any grounds for objections.

Nelson McCann had moved back to Plattsburgh from St. Louis when his father died. He was a lawyer, but once he got into the swing of running his family farm he decided to stay put. Personally, I suspected there were other reasons he wanted to live in Plattsburgh, and the biggest reason was sitting across the table from me, slurping her coffee. Aunt

Patti and Nelson were the same age, around thirty-one, and they had been dating for several weeks now. At first it freaked me out that she was getting serious.

"April, I promise you, we're taking it very slow," she had said the morning after I walked in on them pretty much in each other's laps watching TV. "I've been alone too long, and I'm just too mature—ahem—to leap headfirst into a serious relationship."

Even though I snickered at the thought of Aunt Patti being mature, I believed her. Way back when my parents were killed in a freak horse-training accident—the reason for my long, long dread of anything having to do with riding a horse—Aunt Patti moved in to take care of me. I was only four years old, and she basically changed everything about her life and her plans to raise me. Instead of going to graduate school to study botany, she opened a flower shop, Room for Blooms, in Plattsburgh and moved us into a little house not far from the center of town. We hung out, we talked, and we got along great, almost like cousins or friends. Aunt Patti had a few weird habits— what grown-up doesn't?—but I counted on her completely. To think of her getting serious with a guy was not yet on my radar. I wasn't ready to deal with that major a change, and she knew it.

Now she was sitting like she always did at the little table we had in the kitchen, hunched over the newspaper. Aunt Patti always spent some time looking over the page that listed the weddings and deaths. Because she was a florist, a big part of her job was doing the floral arrangements for weddings, funerals, and other major events. She didn't call people to drum up business but, as she said, "I just like to know who's doing what around here." Actually, Aunt Patti had done the flowers for Mr. McCann's funeral, and for a huge wedding over the summer. Things had quieted down for her since then, which explained why she was so relaxed.

"You know, Nelson was wondering if either of us knew anyone who might be able to take your place on the farm now that school's starting up," Aunt Patti said. "This is probably a bad time to ask you, but maybe just put it in the back of your mind for now."

I ate breakfast mechanically, not really tasting anything but knowing I had to get through the bowl or my stomach would hurt before lunch. As I got ready to leave the house, Aunt Patti stood up and put her hands on my shoulders.

"Have fun today, babe," she said. "By the way, I like the way you did your hair."

"Thanks." Instead of throwing my wad of brown curly

tangles into a messy bun, I had brushed it out the night before and made two braids. I was sure a couple of my friends would make cracks but, hey, it was the first day.

"How about Shawn?" I said, amazed that Shawn had popped into my head just then. Shawn Clarke was a veteran who had returned from the Iraq war in a wheelchair. I had met him at the library over the summer when he was studying for college admission tests, and Rainy Day and I had rescued him from his trailer when Plattsburgh flooded back in May.

"I know he's in a wheelchair and all," I added quickly, "but you know, he's incredibly strong."

Aunt Patti looked at me. "It hadn't even occurred to me to ask Shawn," she said. "It's an idea. But you should get going now. It's seven-nineteen."

I laughed and left, banging out the back screen door.

"Don't worry about Rainy Day, April," Aunt Patti called to me from the porch. "I'll come home at lunchtime to check on him this first day."

Lowell was waiting for me around the front of the house on the sidewalk, but I made one quick dash to Rainy Day. He was grazing in the dewy wet grass of our small paddock.

"Bye, boy," I said. "I'll miss you today."

He shoved his brown muzzle toward my hip, as if checking to see whether I had any treats for him. I scratched him extra hard under his chin. "Nothing this morning. Just a backpack full of loose-leaf paper." Rainy Day lifted his head up and away from me, took a step to the side, and then bowed to the fresh green grass at his front hooves.

Lowell was still waiting for me out front. "Hey, April," he said.

"Morning," I said. "Well, here we go." We fell in step just like we had for years.

"I wonder what Kruger is going to say to kick off the year," Lowell said.

"Oh, my guess is the usual. A reminder to be yourself, to act with integrity, not to cheat, and not to do the stupid stuff that certain people will do no matter what Kruger says."

Lowell laughed. "Sounds about right."

Soon we met up with a bunch of kids heading toward Plattsburgh Middle School. That human stream merged into a bigger river, and eventually we were a huge tide of kids flowing into the double doors of the building, which were both wide open on the first day. One of the English teachers stood at the door, greeting everyone. Left and right, people were saying hi to friends they hadn't seen all summer, pausing to exchange excited greetings and comments about hair, outfits, and things like that. A math teacher acted like a traffic cop to get us to keep walking into the auditorium, where we had our first assembly. I moved toward my seat and ended up having to climb over the kid in the seat next to mine. I had completely forgotten about him, but it must have been the new kid, Matthew. He didn't even look up as I took a giant step over his bony kneecaps. As I got settled in my seat, I noticed that he seemed to be totally concentrating on a small leatherbound book. When I got a closer look, I saw that it was a pocket dictionary. The cover was really worn, and the pages were smudged at the corners, as if they had been turned hundreds of times by slightly dirty fingers. Every so often he gave a quick darting glance up toward the podium, but then quickly returned to the dictionary. I noticed his hands and face were very pale, which seemed especially out of place at the end of summer, when everyone was their most tan. His shirt was untucked and he had a severe case of bed head.

"Hi," I said, feeling too awkward not acknowledging each other's presence. He didn't reply. I dipped my head forward and sort of turned back up to catch his eye.

"Hey. Are you Matthew?"

He closed the book over one finger and leaned back in his seat as if to get farther away from me.

"Hello," he said. "Yes, my name is Matthew R. Heisman. But you can call me Matt."

His voice sounded a little robotic, and the way he introduced himself was certainly unusual, but his eyes were shiny and brown, and he had a cute smile. A *very* cute smile.

"I'm April. April Helmbach. I saw your name on our class list."

Matt seemed to be extremely distracted by all the kids talking and getting into their seats. His eyes roamed every which way as I was talking. I don't think he looked directly back at me for more than a split second. I figured he was nervous, it being his first day in a new school and all.

"This is usually a pretty short assembly," I said. "Just the pep talk and corny jokes from Kruger, the principal. Did you just move here?"

"No," he replied. "We moved to Plattsburgh last Thursday at four."

I was too confused by his answer to say anything. It took me another minute to understand that he meant that he hadn't *literally just this second* moved to our town, but by then we were being told to quiet down.

All through Kruger's speech, I found myself sneaking looks at Matt. There was something about him I couldn't put my finger on, something unusual, but also—I don't know—innocent. I saw that he was nervously drumming his right leg up and down. He could hardly sit still.

When Kruger was all done, everyone started gathering their things to head off to their lockers and first period. Matt stood up and stashed his dictionary in the back pocket of his jeans. Then, like everyone else, he slung his backpack over his shoulder and started shuffling out toward the aisle. I tapped him on the shoulder and it looked like he was about to leap up to the ceiling, he was so startled.

"I'm sorry," I said. "I just wanted to let you know that if you have any questions or anything, you can always find me. Maybe look for me and my friends at lunch, too."

"Thanks," he said. "I will do that. Thank you."

He raised his palm in my direction and turned into the hall, where I soon lost sight of him in the onrush of kids.

Chapter

I didn't see Matt again until third-period geometry. He was sitting in the back row, looking down at his dictionary. When the bell rang, he put it in his backpack and opened a spiral notebook. Our geometry teacher, Mr. Barnholtz, was one of those no-nonsense types who doesn't spend a second, even on the first day back, sharing stories about summer break. Right away we were reviewing whatever we could remember about obtuse and acute angles, polygons, mathematical definitions, and basic vocabulary about proofs. Mr. Barnholtz would ask a question, call on someone who would hem and haw (none of us studied that much geometry in earlier grades), and then call on Matt, who had his hand up and answered every single question correctly. Eventually, kids started turning around in their seats whenever he spoke. A few kids rolled their eyes, but the thing I noticed was how Matt didn't seem to be self-conscious about what was happening. He didn't seem embarrassed or apologetic, and he didn't act cool and above-it-all, the way some kids do to not seem like teacher's pets when they happen to know stuff. It was like he was just answering questions because he knew the answers, not to prove anything at all. No big deal to him, but it definitely stood out to me.

The bell rang and Matt jumped out of his seat in alarm.

"Hey," I said. "What have you got next?"

"English."

"Me too. It's just across the hall."

I followed him to the back row of class and noticed that once he got all his books out, he sat resting his chin in his hands so that he could put his fingers in his ears. I knew what he was doing—muffling the horribly loud bell that drove us from place to place all day long. He sat perfectly still.

"Hi, April," said a voice next to me. I had been so caught up in watching Matt, I hadn't even noticed my friend Ruby.

"Oh, hey, Ruby. What's up?"

"Not much. I'm not ready for this, though."

"For what?"

"This..." She glanced around the whole classroom as if to suggest that she meant everything in the entire building in general. I laughed.

"I know, me neither."

"Who's that guy on your other side?" she asked.

"His name's Matt Heisman. He's new this year."

Ruby raised her eyebrows and smiled, which I took to mean that she considered him worth talking to. I looked at Matt, thinking I would introduce them, but he was looking down and had his ears plugged. It didn't seem like a good time.

The bell rang, and our teacher, Mrs. Fremont, came in and asked us to pull out *Into Thin Air*, which had been our summer reading. In this class Matt said hardly anything at all, but he listened closely to the discussion. We talked about the values of the people who spent thousands of dollars so that they could say they had climbed the tallest peak in the world. We talked about the role of the sherpas, who carried all the supplies, and about the author's decisions along the way. At one point Mrs. Fremont called on Matt, probably because he hadn't said a peep, and asked him whether he would have turned back when it was clear the excursion was getting too risky.

"I mean," Mrs. Fremont said, "how would you feel knowing that you were about to throw away a huge investment and maybe never again have a chance to try to summit?"

Mrs. Fremont looked perfectly friendly, but Matt

seemed very uncomfortable. He sat silently as people started fidgeting.

"There's no right or wrong answer," Mrs. Fremont said. "I'm just wondering."

"I have no idea," Matt said finally. "I have no idea how I would feel in that situation."

Mrs. Fremont looked sort of puzzled, but I was relieved that she let it go and called on somebody else. Ruby passed me a note. I unfolded the torn square of loose leaf paper and read:

What's with him?

I wrote back hastily:

Nothing. It's just his first day.

I knew that wasn't exactly true—something about Matt *was* different—but I also knew that it was true enough for now.

By the time 3:10 rolled around, I was tired. I had homework in every subject, and I had to figure out what to do about joining a team. I saw Lowell by his locker and stopped by to see if he wanted to walk home.

"Can't," he said. "Cross-country."

"How's it going anyway?" I said, dropping my two-ton backpack for a minute.

"Great. I really like it. It's cool getting so far away every day and not having to think about anything except matching the footsteps of the guy in front of you. Plus, I like the feeling when it's done. You're tired, but in a good way. I mean, your brain's not tired, only your legs. I only wish it wasn't so hot. Some guys puke every single practice."

"Gross."

"Yeah, I know."

I picked up my backpack because it seemed like Lowell was in a hurry.

"What about clubs?" I asked. "Are you doing any this year?"

"I think I'm going to give the newspaper a try," he said. "Fremont's the advisor and she suggested it. She said anyone with as strong opinions as I have ought to be on the newspaper. I'm not sure if that was a compliment or not."

I laughed and turned to go. "All right, well, see you. Same time tomorrow morning?"

"Cool. See you, April."

At home, I headed straight for the backyard and saw Rainy Day on the other side of the paddock from where I had left him that morning. As soon as he saw me, he trotted in my direction and we met in the middle. He buried his nose under my arm, and I patted his head and scratched behind his ears.

"That's the longest we've ever gone not seeing each other all day," I said. "How was it? Did you miss me?"

He play-nibbled at my sleeve, half closed his eyes, and pricked his ears forward.

"Me too," I said, throwing my arms around his neck. "How are we going to get through this?"

Rainy Day looked away and bent down to the grass as if suddenly preoccupied with grazing. I know it sounds crazy, but for a second he reminded me of the new boy, Matt. It was like Rainy Day knew he was unable to figure out the human world—why had I suddenly disappeared all day, when I had always been around before?—so he would just leave it be and go about his own business. Which made sense for a horse, but not for a kid.

"I wonder if we could go out for a short ride before I get started on homework," I said. I checked my watch and decided there was time. "C'mon, boy. It won't be long, but it'll do us good."

I led Rainy Day into the barn and brushed the day's dust and dirt off his back. I laid on his well-worn saddle blanket and threw the saddle over it. All of his tack, I noticed, was looking sort of old and tattered. The stripes on the blanket had faded, and the saddle was scuffed and scratched so much, you could hardly make out the decorative etchings around the horn and down along the sides. All of the equipment had been put in storage ten years ago when my parents died. They had been horse trainers and the owners of a prominent stable in Plattsburgh. Aunt Patti had so much to do and think about when they died that she wanted everything having to do with horses out of sight. Because of my extreme fear of riding and horses, it never looked like I would want to claim the equipment.

But then came the truck accident and Rainy Day. The old tack was pulled out of storage, I learned to ride, and discovered that I was "born to the barn," as Marty, my riding mentor, said. Right from the start, Rainy Day and I seemed to have one adventure after another. The rides we took in that first month, when we faced floodwaters, debris, and knee-deep mud, probably caused more wear and tear on the equipment than anything from back in my parents' day. Even though I tried to get all the accumulated dirt off, you would never mistake Rainy Day's tack for that of a fresh, performing rodeo horse. Everything functioned, but

I would have loved to see Rainy Day all decked out in smooth new leather and a halter with shiny silver accents. On the other hand, it was complicated, because that old gear was among my last physical links to my parents. These were things they had touched, things that mattered to them in their day-to-day lives. A part of me didn't want to replace any of it. Kind of like my mom's old horse books, like *Black Beauty* and the others I had read for the first time that summer.

When we came home after that first-day-of-school ride, I took extra time with his grooming. I brushed out Rainy Day's bangs and tail, and even polished his hooves. At that point I knew I had crossed the line between responsible care and procrastination, but that didn't stop me. It was only the first day of school, I told myself, and there would be plenty of time to do homework after dinner. Leaving Rainy Day clean and comfortable, and yanking fresh hay out of his feed bracket, I walked back over to the house. I pulled off my barn boots, left them outside on the porch, and dragged my backpack in behind me.

"Wow, it smells amazing in here," I said, reaching down to pet Chase, who was jumping up on my legs. Aunt Patti was in the kitchen, her back to the door. I came up behind her and peered over her shoulder. "Whatcha making?"

"Nothing fancy," she said. "We've got so many tomatoes coming ripe, I can't keep up. Spaghetti sauce uses tons. I think you're smelling the garlic and herbs."

Aunt Patti had a big, overflowing garden in a fenced-in, sunny area of our two-acre yard. She grew most of the vegetables, herbs, and berries we ate all summer, and canned the surplus for the winter.

"Anything ready now?" I asked, looking around for something to pick up and eat. "I'm starving."

Aunt Patti turned and smiled. She had a knife in one hand and her other hand was shiny and wet. She leaned forward to peck me on the cheek.

"How was the first day? And yes, check the fridge. I made some deviled eggs. Please let Chase out."

I let out Chase, fixed a plate, and sat down at the table. This was one of my favorite times of day. Coming home from school and snacking and chatting with Aunt Patti, I felt like we had this safe little place where it was just the two of us and we could talk about anything. I told her a little bit about my classes and teachers, and I told her about Matt.

"Hmmm . . . " she said. "He sounds like an interesting person."

I shrugged. *Interesting* was what an adult would say, for sure, but did not seem to exactly capture Matt. Not that I knew a better word. We fell into a comfortable silence while she worked and I did my math homework.

"You can set the table, April," she said about a half hour later. "Remember we're three."

"What?"

"Remember I mentioned this morning that Nelson was coming over?"

I had forgotten, of course, and felt a little annoyed that I would have to be social after my first day of school. Aunt Patti looked away, as if she half expected me to be annoyed but didn't want me to be. So I kept my feelings unspoken. And the truth was that I had worked for Nelson all summer. I liked him a lot. He had already started to feel a little like family.

"Kitchen or dining room?" I said.

"Whichever you'd prefer," she said, arranging sliced radishes and cherry tomatoes on big bowl-shaped lettuce leaves. "Maybe since you've got your books spread out, it'd be easier in the dining room."

Nelson arrived around seven. In jeans and a polo shirt he looked much younger than thirty-one, more like twenty-six. His skin had tanned from a summer of farming, and his clear gray eyes were lit as usual with happy energy. He handed Aunt Patti one of those enormous one-pound bars of chocolate and gave her a big smooch on the cheek. He handed me a paperback with a blue ribbon tied around it.

"*To Kill a Mockingbird*?" I read.

"That happens to be the very first book that made me think seriously about life," he said. "I want you to read it and tell me what you think."

"But what if I'm not ready to think seriously about life?" I joked.

"In that case, just read it for fun and don't think about life at all," he said, a deadpan expression on his face.

Chapter

"It smells great in here, Patti."

"Thank you," she said. "Dinner's all ready. Let's eat."

Over a steaming bowl of linguine with fresh tomato sauce, Nelson told us that he was genuinely worried about managing his farm without Lowell and me helping every day.

"But I suppose you guys have to go to school and do homework and that whole routine, right?" he said.

"Yeah, not being Amish," I said. "Although sometimes I think I'd consider converting."

I was referring to the people I had gotten to know over the summer and now considered my friends. They were a family called the Rhinestats, and they practiced a religion where kids stopped going to school at fourteen in order to work on the farm with their parents. Mr. Rhinestat had helped rescue the quarter horse foal, JP, which was born right around the time that old Mr. McCann, Nelson's father, died. The foal had spooked and run all the way to the Rhinestat place, where I eventually found him.

"But seriously, about your situation," I said. "I can still work some afternoons, like Fridays, and also a bit on weekends some. But for the real work during the week, I was thinking about Shawn. Remember him?"

"Of course I remember him," Nelson said. "Shawn Clarke. But..."

"But he's in a wheelchair?" I said. "Is that what you were going to say?" I grated a little more Parmesan on my linguine and waited.

"Well, yeah," Nelson said.

"Don't you remember how incredibly strong he is? From the waist up he's like an iron man, and he has that, like, super all-terrain wheelchair. Or he did, before it floated away in the flood. But I'm sure he's got a new one by now."

"It's true," Aunt Patti said. "Remember how he pulled himself up onto Rainy Day's back behind April, when she found him stranded in the doorway of his trailer during the flood?"

"Wasn't he applying to college or something? How do we know he's around?" Nelson said, clearly intrigued by the possibility.

"Not till January, I think," I said. "It's worth a call anyway. I think he and his mom are renting a place in those

Valley Apartments. But you can count on me tomorrow anyway."

"I'll look into it," Nelson said. "Thanks for the tip, April."

Aunt Patti and Nelson went on to talk about her day at Room for Blooms, and I spaced out for a while. When I tuned back in, Aunt Patti was looking at me questioningly, as if expecting an answer.

"Sorry?" I said. "What?"

"I was telling Nelson about that new boy you mentioned. Matt, I think you said his name was?"

So I described what I had observed about Matt, especially about how he answered the question about "just moving here." Nelson thought for a moment while Aunt Patti and I talked about what homework I had left that night.

"It sounds like this kid might have Asperger's," Nelson said finally.

"Really?" Aunt Patti said.

"What's that?" I asked.

"Well, back when I was a public defender, there was this guy in our office who called himself an Aspie, which many people with this condition do. It's a jokey sort of shorthand for Asperger's syndrome, kind of his lighthearted way to break the ice. So we would know that he viewed his condition objectively and with a sense of humor, I think."

"Lowell kind of does that with his inability to play games with balls," I said.

"You're probably right," Nelson said. "Anyway, eventually we learned that it's a condition related to autism."

"Whoa!" I said. "Isn't that those kids who can't speak, and do kind of disturbing things like bang their heads on the wall?"

"In extreme cases, April, yes," Aunt Patti said. "But—"

"But autism and Asperger's have a whole range of behavior and symptoms," Nelson said. "Some people with Asperger's can be extremely socially awkward. And sometimes very childlike in the way they take things literally."

"That definitely sounds like Matt," I said, swiping a piece of bread around the bottom of my bowl to get every drop of cheesy olive oil. Aunt Patti chimed in to the discussion.

"The point is that there are many, many different kinds of ways people can have Asperger's, April. They are often very intelligent, and very sensitive to things like sudden noises or changes in light. I'm thinking of what you said about how Matt jumped when the bell rang. Please don't feed Chase under the table, Nelson," Aunt Patti said.

"Yeah," I said. "Only Lowell gets to do that." Lowell was forever sneaking food to Chase.

"Anyway," Aunt Patti said, "this is all speculation on our part, April. Let's keep this confidential, and just be nice to this boy. I'm sure you were. He must be very high functioning to be in public school, at any rate, so you can assume he'll adjust."

It was a lot to digest, all that stuff about Matt and Asperger's. More than I really could think about just then. I cleared my plate and excused myself to my room. There I shut the door and got down to homework. Eventually I could hear laughter and murmurs from the other room and knew that Aunt Patti seemed like a happier person now that Nelson was in her life.

Later on, right before I fell asleep, a slice of light opened into the room and I saw Aunt Patti's silhouette approach my bed. She leaned over and stared down at me.

"April, honey?" she whispered. "Are you still up?"

"Barely," I murmured.

She sat down by my waist and put her hand on my forehead.

"I just wanted one more hug," she said. "The first day of school is a big deal. Is there anything else I should know going into tomorrow?"

"I don't think so," I said sleepily.

"There's something else I wanted to mention but I forgot," Aunt Patti said. "Your birthday. Have you given any thought about what you might want? Or how you want to celebrate?"

On September eighteenth, I would turn fourteen.

"I'm too tired to think about it now."

"I know, but if you want to have a party or anything, we ought to be thinking about it. Also, your grandparents bought a bond for you on your birthday ten years ago and you'll be getting a nice little chunk of money from that."

"Define 'nice little chunk,'" I said.

"I think it could be around several hundred dollars," Aunt Patti said, pausing for the amount to sink in. "We'll need to think about whether to save it, or spend it, or maybe work out a combination."

We hugged one last time and Aunt Patti left the room and closed the door. I heard her walking around the house, turning off lights and then going into her own room. One thing I especially liked about our house was that you could hear everything from everywhere. It was a small one-story bungalow, with two bedrooms down a narrow hallway, a living room, a dining room, and a kitchen. We had small porches at the front and back, and a big two-acre yard that had plenty of room for Rainy Day's one-horse barn, a fenced-in paddock, and Aunt Patti's gardens. "A little house on a lotta land," is how Aunt Patti described it.

As I lay in the still house, it occurred to me that I could use some of the bond money to replace Rainy Day's tack and some of our grubbier tools and supplies. On the other hand, the thought of not using the equipment once used by my parents didn't feel right. I sighed and imagined removing all the thoughts in my head and stuffing them into a drawer for the night. They'd be there in the morning, but for now, they were in the way of sleep.

The next day at lunch, I wound up at a table with Lowell, Matt, Ruby, and the new girl, Monica Shinkel. The mingled smells of tuna fish, Tater Tots, and the hot lunch option (always a mystery) swirled around us as kids carried their trays through the aisles and found places to sit. Matt had been all alone at the end of a table when the rest of us joined him. I tried not to stare as he carefully removed the paper from his straw. He was doing it systematically, first removing the tip and then pushing the rest of the wrapper into an evenly spaced accordion. Nobody else seemed to be paying any attention because Ruby was asking Monica all about how she got to our school. She explained her arrival in one gushing try.

"Well, I used to go to elementary school in West County, which is the boonies of St. Louis, but then my dad got transferred to an office in Rolla, and Plattsburgh is halfway between St. Louis and Rolla, so we moved here so his commute wouldn't be so bad if my mom kept her job, which is in St. Louis."

"Jeez," Lowell said. "I guess that makes sense."

"So, what are the kids like here?" Monica asked, looking around the cafeteria. She had long blond hair and blue eyes. It was the kind of hair Ruby envied, naturally streaked and perfectly straight. Ruby's hair was dark blond and frizzy, which every so often she convinced her mom to let her highlight and get straightened.

"I don't know," Lowell said. "Plattsburgh's kind of mixed. Some farmers, some local business types, some commuters, and at certain times of the year, there are migrant families that come through to do the harvests. Their kids come to school for a couple months and then leave."

"There's this boy in ninth grade, Bryan Lim," I said. "His parents own the one Chinese restaurant in town."

"Pretty much typical middle Missouri," Lowell said.

"Like my dad, he works for the roads and engineering crew. My mom goes into St. Louis to work."

"And I live with my aunt," I added. "She's a florist. But her boyfriend was a lawyer and now is a farmer."

It seemed like Matt was listening, but he didn't say anything. He was nibbling his sandwich into a perfect square. Monica finished off her carton of milk and put it down. She was staring hard at Matt. I could tell she was trying to figure out whether what he was doing was for real or a put-on.

"Well," she said, shaking her hair away from her eyes, "I'm a quarter Native American, a quarter French, and half German."

Lowell burst out laughing, and Monica looked offended.

"Sorry," he said. "When I said 'mixed,' I meant kind of what people around here do, not exactly their ethnic makeup or whatever."

Monica shrugged. "Whatever," she said, and I hoped someone would change the subject, which had turned a little weird, even for people like us who tended to say random things for no apparent reason.

Suddenly Matt's face lit up all happy. "I am two-sixteenths Polish, two-sixteenths German, four-sixteenths Russian, and eight-sixteenths Irish," he said.

None of us knew what to say to this. Matt had taken an already odd conversation and made it even odder. I knew there were kids—Monica was obviously one of them—who kept track of their heritage in pretty precise detail, and often with pride, but Matt's fractions were over-the-top. Assuming Matt was joking, Lowell burst out laughing, as did Monica and Ruby. I looked at Matt and he seemed amused and relieved to be part of the conversation. He even started to laugh, too. But after Lowell and the others stopped laughing, Matt continued to guffaw as if what he had said was the most hilarious thing ever. By then the others were looking at him in a way that made me uncomfortable. Monica yanked on Ruby's sleeve and whispered something in her ear, then laughed in a mean way. At least I thought it was mean. Especially when I remembered what Nelson suspected about Matt.

Like a faucet turned off, Matt's laughter stopped instantly and he went back to his food.

"So, Monica," Ruby asked, "what's your fall sport?"

"I don't know," she said. "Don't we have until, like, Monday or something to decide? I am so totally bad at everything."

"You could run," Lowell said. "Cross-country's hard, but it's only running, and anyone can run. None of that balls, arms, and sticks in your face stuff, which all suck."

Ruby and I laughed, knowing how much Lowell hated all the normal sports like soccer and baseball that he could never play to save his life. Ruby encouraged Monica to come out for field hockey, but Monica looked doubtful.

"I don't know, either," I said to make her feel better. "I'm going into the athletic department on Monday to talk about substituting horseback riding for a sport. I know girls who do dance outside of school and get P.E. credit. And this one kid fences. They make exceptions all over the place."

"Yeah, well, I don't know if I do anything that would even qualify as an exception," Monica said.

Down at the end of the table, Matt came alive again and drew out a thick pack of cards from the leg pocket of his cargoes. A crossed rubber band held them together, and when he took off the rubber band, Lowell gave a shout.

"Wizard cards! Dude, you play Wizard? I haven't played since fifth grade." He got up and moved across the table from Matt. After the mean whispering Monica had done to mock Matt, I could have hugged Lowell for being sincere.

Matt smiled. "I always carry a couple of sets around.

41

Today I have my black-and-red deck and my goblin deck."

Monica rolled her eyes and scooted as far as possible from Matt's end of the table. Everyone our age knew about Wizard. It had been all the rage among the boys for most of grade school. I used to play with Lowell just because he constantly begged me to, but my heart was never in it. It was funny how Matt and Lowell could connect over Wizard. Matt passed a deck to Lowell to check out while he examined his own.

"Dude," Lowell said, "I don't think we have time for a game right now, the bell's going to ring any second." At this, Matt looked horrified. "I'm sorry," Lowell said, thinking he had hurt Matt's feelings. "We can play some other time for sure. Okay? Maybe on Monday at lunch if we eat fast and start right away."

Matt hastily rebanded the Wizard cards and slipped them back into his pocket. I could see his dictionary bulging in his rear pocket as he slung his backpack over one shoulder and dashed away to bus his tray.

As the rest of us got up to leave, I pulled Lowell aside.

"I don't think Matt looked that way because you were putting the game off," I said. "You told him the bell was about to ring, and he hates that bell. I mean, I noticed yesterday that he seems to really dislike it."

Lowell looked at me like I was crazy, but I left it at that. "Just trust me on this," I said, knowing I would say more later.

Chapter

That afternoon I went straight home, changed into old work boots, and went into the kitchen. I got an apple out of the fridge and cut it into wedges. I put them in an empty yogurt container and carried them out the back door. I stopped by the barn to get Rainy Day's lead, then went out to find him. It took me a few minutes, because he was standing in the shade in the far corner of his paddock. One of our neighbor's cats, Lady Jane, was lying along a branch overlooking him. She had her eyes closed. It seemed like Rainy Day was watching the hanging laundry flap behind the house where Lady Jane lived.

"Hey, boy," I said, walking toward him and shaking the apples so he would know I hadn't come empty-handed. "How was day two on your own? Did Aunt Patti stop by for a visit? Hey, Lady Jane. Are you here keeping Rainy Day company?"

Rainy Day turned his head and took a few slow steps in my direction. I patted his head and all around his ears. I lay an apple chunk in the palm of my hand and held it up to his muzzle. He lipped it into his mouth and started chewing. As he ate, I looked him over carefully. A small hairless pink patch of scar tissue was all that remained from the injuries he had suffered in May, although somewhere in his mind, I wondered if he carried memories of the sudden jolt and pain. I had not known what Rainy Day was like before the accident, but I knew how calm and gentle he was now. Had the trauma made him more capable of handling stress? It was hard to know. I understood that horses needed to be exposed to all kinds of sounds and sensations in order to learn how to stay calm and in control no matter what was going on around them. And since then, Rainy Day had proven his poise in all kinds of crazy situations— riding through floodwaters, rescuing a cat, and chasing down a runaway foal. Nothing seemed to spook him.

When the apple was all gone, I attached the lead and took him over to the barn. Rainy Day stomped a foot and swished his tail as if to let me know he was excited to do something. He stood very still, on his best behavior while I got him ready to ride over to the McCann place.

We trotted most of the way there. As we approached the well-loved farm, I let Rainy Day break into a canter. I pulled him back to a walk at the roadside mailbox, which had been surrounded by irises throughout May and some of June. Before Nelson moved back, the mailbox had been neglected and off-kilter. Now, freshly repaired and weeded, it stood straight and tall.

"You're excited to see Hannah, aren't you?" I said, drawing in the reins to turn into the driveway.

Rainy Day blew air out of his lips in agreement and slowed to a walk. I led him around to the back of the house toward the barn. His ears pricked forward at the sound of Hannah's loud neigh. Hannah was a quarter horse mare. She had been a favorite of old Mr. McCann's, and now she was a favorite of Nelson's. Back in July she had a foal, JP, who was a couple of months old. I had spent most of the summer here at the McCann place, doing chores and helping to train JP.

Rainy Day nickered back to Hannah. At the paddock fence, I got off, undid his saddle and bridle, and set him free to socialize with his old friend. I turned to lay the tack over a fence rail.

"April!" I heard a voice call behind me. It was Marty Smitherman, one of the best trainers in Plattsburgh. Out of friendship for Mr. McCann, he had taken an interest in JP. Out of respect for my parents, he had taken an interest in me. If it hadn't been for Marty, I never would have learned so much—so fast—about horses and riding. Horse-wise, it was like the ten years between when my parents died and now had never happened. I couldn't imagine how I had ever hated and feared horses as much as I did.

"Hey, Marty, what's up?" I said, turning and running over to the barn door.

"We miss you around here, that's what's up," he said, wiping the sweat off his forehead with a bandanna and leaning on the handle of a heavy shovel. "I came over to check on our young friend," he said, indicating JP. "I'm afraid that critter is going to get into all kinds of bad habits without you to straighten him out. His mama and Rainy Day spoil him. They think he's cute."

"He is cute," I said. "Where is he? Oh, there, I see him."

JP was racing around the paddock not too far from Hannah and Rainy Day. Every few steps, he bucked, kicking his heels back for sheer pleasure. I couldn't help but smile. He was getting bigger and bigger, but he still played around like he had from his first days.

Marty saw me watching them. "See how much fun you could be having if you didn't go to school?"

"Don't remind me, Marty," I said. "It's hard enough as it is."

"Well, then, maybe shoveling manure will help you feel better about things," he joked, passing me the shovel.

47

"You bet," I said. "Is Nelson around?"

"He is. That man has plans," Marty said. "He's over in the outbuilding on the other side of the main house, seeing about the soundness of the roof. Seems he's thinking of starting up raising goats, of all things."

"Goats?"

Marty laughed, following me into the first stall, where I began clearing out dirty hay and heaping it into a wheelbarrow. "Seems it takes a city-slicker lawyer type to figure out that what St. Louis restaurants need is goat cheese. He's been surveying the property all week with the idea of fencing off pastures just for goats. They take the grass down to just about nothing, leave nothing for horses. A goat might as well be a lawn mower."

"Goats?"

"April, you said that already," Marty joked.

This was the first I had heard of the plan.

"I guess I thought he had his hands pretty full around here with a couple of horses, chickens, some geese, and a pig," I said, packing down the contents of the wheelbarrow with the back of the shovel so I could fit more in. Marty was leaning against the half-door of the stall. "Not to mention a couple of ducks."

"Yeah, well, that's nice and all, but Nelson wants a

future here," Marty said. "A future as a farmer means finding a market for what he grows or raises, and Nelson's a smart man. You can bet if he's deciding on goats, it's because there's a market for what he can do with them. Me, I'm all about horses, and I told him so."

"Hmm," I said.

"Well," Marty said, pushing off the wall and shambling toward the barn door, "I'm gonna go check Hannah's rear left leg. She's been standing and moving kinda funny."

When I finished mucking out Hannah's stall, I refilled her water and food buckets and spread fresh hay on the ground. A nail sticking out of the wall caught my eye, and I found a hammer and hammered it back in so it wouldn't catch on either of the horses. Then I fed and watered the chickens and the geese. Next I filled Old Moses's trough from the slop bucket Nelson kept outside the kitchen, and which he loaded with scraps after every meal just like his dad used to do. Finally, I took the long lead and ran out to JP. At first he tried to jump away from me, but one sharp hiss from me and he submitted. We spent a little while in the ring, practicing turns, reverses, starting, and stopping.

"Good boy," I said, feeding him one of the alfalfa cubes I kept in my pocket for training. He nibbled it up gratefully, and I unfastened the rope and let him go back to romping. "Off you go."

JP ran straight to Hannah, and I turned to see if I could find Nelson. He was sitting on the porch looking toward the road, his feet up on the railing just like his dad used to do. He smiled and waved me over.

"Go get a drink, April," he said. "You must be dying of thirst."

I found an orange soda in the fridge and took a seat next to him. We both watched as a pickup truck zoomed by on the dirt road, leaving a rooster tail of dry yellow dust behind it.

"Everything okay out there?" he asked, indicating the direction of the barn.

I snapped open the can and nodded. "Mm-hmm. Marty said something about one of Hannah's legs, but he's on top of that. Everything else is fine. Rainy Day sure is happy to see those guys."

"How'd he weather your being gone these last two days?" Nelson said.

I shrugged. "Eh. I'm not so sure. He's got to be lonely. I'm wondering if I ought to let him come over here during school. Or something else. I don't know." I took a long gulp of soda.

Nelson didn't reply. In fact, he seemed to change the subject.

"So I got through to Shawn today," he said.

"You did? How is he?" I hadn't seen Shawn since May. He had so much to do after his trailer got flooded, what with studying and getting himself settled in a new home.

"He's doing great," Nelson said, crumpling his can with one hand and tossing it behind us into the blue recycling bin he kept there. "Same old wise guy. He's not starting classes until January, and he says he's willing to give farmwork a try. He's going to stop by tomorrow, as a matter of fact. Says he's not going to turn down a chance at making some money before college."

"Cool," I said. We sat quietly for a moment. I knew I should be getting up to head home, but this was the first I had sat down since school was out, and it was pretty nice on that porch. Just like summer.

"By the way, Nelson, goats?"

Nelson laughed. "I guess you talked to Marty?"

"She saw me, all right," Marty said, coming around from the back of the house. "Somebody's gotta talk some horse sense into you, and it might as well be April."

Nelson laughed and leaned toward me conspiratorially. "Seems Marty doesn't care much for my plan."

"Who do you think you are, is all I wonder," Marty said. "Heidi? Old Joe wouldn't stand for it."

"Old Joe, I mean my dad, couldn't make this place pay in the last ten years or so," Nelson said, more seriously than before. "I don't have to tell you that, Marty. This is no economy for the small farmer. At least, the small farmer who doesn't find a place to wedge himself—or herself—into."

Nelson was right. Marty made a good living stabling horses for people in St. Louis. They would always want to keep horses and never would have the time to do all the grooming and care a horse needed. On the other hand, old Mr. McCann had let his farm droop and sag into a kind of useless old-fashioned relic, a storybook farm. When I met him, the whole farm was a mess. If Nelson didn't do something different, he would never be able to make a living. Then he'd have to move back to St. Louis to work. And then he and Aunt Patti might have to break up. I was beginning to see how all of this was connected to me. The jealous side of me could see that if Nelson's goat scheme failed, I would go back to having Aunt Patti all to myself; the nicer side knew that Aunt Patti's future happiness might depend on Nelson's successful management of the McCann farm.

Marty took off his baseball cap and mopped his forehead with a bandanna. "Well, touché," he said. "Who am I to stand in the way of progress?"

"Well, I guess I'd better get home," I said, although I hated to leave. There was something so nice about the end of a farm day when the chores were done and you could just sit and enjoy knowing that you'd made a whole bunch of animals comfortable. Besides, I knew how content Rainy Day was hanging with Hannah and JP. It made it a little easier that Nelson and Marty got up and kept me company walking over to the paddock.

"I spent a little more time with the new kid, Matt, today," I said as we clunked down the porch steps. "Remember? The kid we talked about at dinner last night?"

"Sure I do. The one I thought sounded like he had Asperger's."

"The thing is, sometimes he seems perfectly normal. And then, out of the blue, he does something or says something or reacts in a way that just seems totally—"

"Not normal," Nelson said, finishing my sentence.

"Yeah." I described the situation with the fractions, and a few other things.

"Just remember," Nelson said, "first of all, every kind of behavior can seem normal to someone because, for them anyway, it *is* normal. And second, Asperger's is a whole set of behaviors that lie on a spectrum."

"What does that mean, exactly?"

"Well, you've heard of a light spectrum, I'm sure."

"Like the rainbow?" I said.

"Exactly. A rainbow shows a spectrum of colors. A range."

"Or like the gaits of a horse?" I added.

"You got it," Nelson said. "The various gaits lie on a spectrum, a range of possible ways a horse can move. What I mean is that you can't pinpoint any one and just say, 'Oh, he's autistic or he has Asperger's so he's always like this or always like that. There's a range of how people with Asperger's can be. And whatever way that is, it's normal for them."

We all heard the telephone ringing and Nelson, after saying bye, dashed back to the house. I whistled for Rainy Day and he came right over. Marty patted his neck and he came up to us. I pulled the saddle blanket off the fence and threw it over Rainy Day's back. Marty cinched the girth for me over on Rainy Day's side, then came around to his head, where I was threading his ears into the bridle.

"You know, I have a buddy in St. Louis who runs one of those equine therapy outfits. You know, where people with various problems are put on horseback."

"I never heard of it," I said, honestly. "But it sounds cool."

"Yeah, it is," Marty said, looking Rainy Day in the eye and rubbing his muzzle. "Horses do people good. Anyway, I don't know anything about this kid you were referring to, but I do know that my buddy has all kinds of kids out there riding. Kids with autism. Kids missing limbs. Kids with cancer. Kids with multiple sclerosis, cerebral palsy, all that."

"How do they do it?" I asked, intrigued. "Actually ride, I mean."

"With lots of human help," Marty said. "And really gentle horses. Kinda like this one here," he added, giving Rainy Day one last friendly slap on his flank. "Listen, I gotta get back to my own place," he said. "You two get along before it gets dark."

"Did you hear that?" I asked Rainy Day. He threw his head up, rearranged his lips around the bit, and stomped a rear leg. I took that for a yes.

Chapter

It made sense that horses could help heal people, I thought as we trotted through the dappled light cast through the leaves. In a way, Rainy Day had healed me of my fear of horses. Right after the accident, I assumed he needed me. But maybe I had needed him more. Or maybe it was that connection that made us so perfect together— we needed each other. But somewhere along the line, need turned into love. We just loved being together. I loved riding, and he loved being ridden. I loved caring for him, and he loved being cared for. As we rode home, it occurred to me that all those feelings—healing, needing, and loving—might somehow be all rolled into one, at least where horses were concerned. As if to echo my thoughts, Rainy Day snorted and picked up speed into a canter.

Later, while in the barn, I stood brushing out the dust and burrs caught in his brown coat. He twitched his skin in places as I made big loops with the currycomb. I sneezed when a cloud of dust drifted into my nose. Rainy Day startled and turned to look at me blamingly.

"Sorry, boy," I said. "But, jeez, do you really have to react to every little thing?"

Of course I knew the answer to this question was a hundred-decibel yes. Right from the beginning, Marty had told me that I had to think of horses as prey animals, which is how they thought of themselves.

"They're always alert for danger," he had said. "A mountain lion, a coyote, anything at all could be after them. At least in their own minds. The two things a horse, any horse, is wired to do are: Be on the lookout at all times and run away. A gentle horse is no less alert, but is trusting enough in his owner not to panic, not to react the way he's designed to react."

I knew this as well as I knew anything, but I still thought how weird and intense it must be to go through life so responsive to every single sound, smell, sight, taste, and touch. Actually, the way I had startled Rainy Day reminded me of the way Matt flinched at the school bell. It seemed terrible that an everyday, routine occurrence should be so disturbing for him and would make him suffer at least a dozen times a day. It would be like Rainy Day having to hear a wolf baying every forty-three minutes. Or worse, like him stepping into a yellow jackets' nest! This was a loaded scenario for me, because it's exactly what happened in the accident that killed my parents. They had been training a young filly when she was stung and reared, and threw my mom. The horse landed with all her weight on an artery in my dad's leg. My mom broke her neck and my dad lost too much blood too quickly to survive. And all because of a panic attack on the part of a horse. I wondered if there were some way to help a kid like Matt not feel so afraid and panicky. If horses could learn to be gentle and calm, what about kids like Matt?

Brushed, cleaned, fed, and offered fresh water, Rainy Day stood in his stall, swishing his tail and chewing oats. I said good night and ran into the kitchen, where Aunt Patti was banging through the pots in a lower cabinet trying to find the skillet she wanted.

"Anything I can do?" I offered, relieved that it was Friday night and the weekend lay ahead.

"Oh, hi, babe," she said. "Sure. Go ahead and set the table and feed Chase. I just need to sauté the snap peas. The rest of dinner's ready. Oh, Ruby called. Lowell, too. They want to see if you can go to a movie later on."

"Could you give me a ride one way or the other?"

"I'd prefer to rather than from, if that's okay," she said. "I need to shower real quick before dinner, though."

After dinner, Aunt Patti and I climbed into our pickup

and drove over to the mall. We talked a little bit about the whole goat plan.

"What do you think about it anyway?" I asked.

"I think it's very cool," Aunt Patti said. "And we've actually talked about cooperating," she added nonchalantly, as if I shouldn't make too much of it.

"Cooperating how?" I pulled down the sun visor to look at myself in the tiny mirror. My damp hair was like a wad of winding brown snakes sprawling around my neck and shoulders. I collected it all in one hand and twisted it into a low, messy bun.

"Well," she began, somewhat hesitantly, "it's still very vague, but somehow combining the stuff I grow in our garden with the products he could offer—goat milk, goat cheese, eggs, you know. We think we could produce enough to sell at the farmers' market in Clayton all summer long, and to supply a handful of restaurants through the winter, assuming I canned what we didn't sell."

"Hmmm." I didn't want to say anything out loud, but it sure did seem like Aunt Patti and Nelson were heading beyond the realm of dating and into the realm of something more serious. A business partnership? You had to be pretty serious about someone if you started thinking about working together. No matter what, it was obvious to me that Aunt Patti and Nelson had a lot in common. I hadn't given much thought to how lonely Aunt Patti might have been out here in Plattsburgh all these years and how happy she was now to be with someone like Nelson.

"But really, April, at this point it's just a fantasy," Aunt Patti said, scanning my face for my initial reaction to this bit of news. "And here we are," she added, pulling up to the curb. "Call me when the movie lets out so I know you're on your way home. Who's picking up?"

"Miz Fran," I said, knowing that Aunt Patti would be relieved to know it was Lowell's mom, so we would be coming right home. "Thanks for the ride. See you," I said, stepping onto the curb and waving bye.

"Bye, hon. Have fun."

It was just about dark by now, and I scanned all the clumps of teenagers for my friends. Everyone was pretty psyched to be out. In Plattsburgh, the first Friday night of the school year is usually pretty rowdy.

"April! Hey!"

I smiled and waved when I saw Lowell standing with Ruby, Monica, and a couple of other kids I didn't recognize. As I walked over, a kid on a skateboard rolled into me and said sorry. He hopped off, tucked it under his arm, and approached another clump of kids.

"Hey, you guys," I said.

"April, this is Nicole," Ruby said. "She plays field hockey with us, so after practice we invited her to come."

"Great. Hi." Nicole and I smiled at each other.

"And this is Tommy," Lowell said. "He runs cross-country."

"Hey," Tommy and I both said at the same time.

"C'mon, we better go in and get tickets," Lowell said. "It's packed tonight."

The six of us walked through the electric sliding doors and went from warm August night to freezing air-conditioned mall-land. All the girls but me started talking about how one of the field hockey coaches was already playing favorites with one of the other eighth graders.

"And it's only because her dad was the head coach at Central, where Ms. G went to high school and played," Monica said.

"Well, I for one am pretty sure I'll be on the bench this whole season," Ruby said.

"You shouldn't assume that," Nicole said. "I mean, that would be so totally unfair if that was the only reason."

I had no opinion on the alleged unfairness of Ms. G the field hockey coach, so I turned to listen in on the boys. But of course Tommy and Lowell were yakking about how impossible that afternoon's run had been and how much they had felt like puking during the repeats up Hanger's Hill. Nothing much for me in that conversation, either, so I just sort of tagged along and said nothing. I was beginning to realize what could happen if I didn't play sports.

Lowell took charge at the box office and got us all tickets. We passed him our share of dollars and he pocketed the cash. Before heading into the theater he and I got in line to buy what we always bought—a box of chocolate-covered raisins for me and gummy candy for him. I found myself staring at the popcorn window all lit up with yellow light, and at the nacho machine with its blinking bulbs. Kids were shouting and yelling orders to one another across the lobby about saving seats, front or back, and on which side. It was noisy, and the whole lobby smelled like popcorn, fake butter, and those fat pink hot dogs, which were twirling on the silver rollers that kept them cooking. The thought crossed my mind: How would Matt handle a scene like this? Did he ever go to the movies like "normal kids"?

Lowell turned away from the counter, took a sip of soda through a straw, and tried to see which theater had the movie we were seeing.

"We should have invited Matt," I said, trying to bring him up without being too obvious.

"Yeah," Lowell said. "He's cool. We should have. Next time."

"What's with him anyway?" Monica said. "He's so bizarre. I swear, he is, like, so totally weird."

"I don't know," I said, trying to think of a way to defend Matt that wouldn't make Monica turn on me, too. "He's just..."

Monica and Ruby both looked at me expectantly. Monica finished my sentence.

"Weird," she said.

Disgusted by Monica, and mad at myself for not saying more, I turned to catch up with Lowell. We passed into the darkness right before they dimmed the lights for the preview.

"Are you really going to get together with him to play Wizard?" I asked as casually as I could. But Lowell and I had been friends too long for that second question to go unnoticed. He looked at me in the dark for a long second before heading across the knees of all the kids in our row. I tried to read his expression, which seemed to be a mixture of suspicion, surprise, and curiosity. We sat down in the seats the others had saved for us just as the previews started blasting. One after another showed fireballs of cars crashing into walls, and gun barrels pointing at scowling guys' temples.

Ruby nudged me to ask if she could stick her hand down into my box of candy, and I nodded. Then I helped myself to her mints. I found myself closing my eyes for most of the previews. By the time our movie started, I was already bored with the action.

The next morning, after doing my chores and turning out Rainy Day, I went online and researched equine therapy. I learned that equine-assisted therapy had been around for a while. It had started in England in the 1960s. Someone realized that calm horses could work wonders for people who suffered from various disorders. And not just by riding them, but by touching them, grooming them, and simply being near them. It was exactly what Marty had said the day before. All those nonverbal ways of communicating got through to people who had limited use of their arms and legs or even no way of speaking. I also saw the place just outside of St. Louis that Marty mentioned people could go for this treatment. It was called Willow Grove Glen. I clicked on their website and saw pictures of the riding ring and the horses they used for their therapy. When I saw that the minimum age for volunteers was fourteen, I practically leaped out of my desk chair. I would be fourteen in a couple of weeks!

When Aunt Patti came home from Room for Blooms after lunch, I began lobbying her to take me to Willow Grove Glen as soon as possible.

"Please, please," I begged. "It's not too far. And I promise I won't ask for a ride on Friday night for at least four months straight."

"Whoa, whoa, whoa, April," she said. "What's this new plan? Slow down, back up, and start from the beginning."

I explained everything Marty had told me, and made her check out the website.

"Well," Aunt Patti said. "We could stop in tomorrow on our way into St. Louis. Remember we were going to have supper at Grandma's? She's been on my case about how long it's been since we've visited."

"That would be great," I said.

"But I can't make any promises about you volunteering," she cautioned. "Can we please just take this one step at a time?"

"One step at a time," I said, backing away, knowing it was time to stop badgering. "Yes, ma'am, one step."

Sometimes the only thing a person can do is flop on her bed on a Saturday afternoon and stare at the dust drifting slowly in the air.

Chapter

Willow Grove Glen turned out to be a plain, unmarked farm tucked into the outskirts of a St. Louis suburb about twenty minutes from Plattsburgh. The houses surrounding it were huge and sprawling, with four-car garages and manicured yards tended by teams of landscapers. As we drove along, Aunt Patti whistled at the development of the area she had known when she was growing up.

"These were all farms back then," she said. "Right around here was a farm stand where we bought our corn and tomatoes all summer long, and I remember—"

"Excuse me, Aunt Patti," I interrupted. "Look, there's the sign."

A tiny painted placard was nailed across a mailbox at the end of a tar-paved driveway. We turned off the main road and wound around a pasture. A riding ring lay on one side of the road, and a long sloping grass meadow on the other. After driving about a quarter mile into the property, we pulled up and parked in front of a large barn. Its foundation was stone, while its outer walls were white-painted wood. Aunt Patti and I got out and looked around for someone.

"I wonder how they've managed to hang on to this place when everything else around here's been developed," Aunt Patti mused.

I ignored her question, being a lot less interested in St. Louis real estate development than in seeing the therapy horses, and soon. Where were they?

"I'll go inside and see if I can find anyone," I said, heading toward a door in the barn.

"I'll hang out here, if that's okay," Aunt Patti said. "It's a gorgeous day."

It was dark and cool compared to outside, and it took me a minute to adjust my eyes to the light. I was standing on a large cobblestone floor. To my left were five or six sunken stalls separated from the cobblestone area by brown wooden half-walls. I walked over to the first stall and peered down. Much to my surprise, I saw a plump, long-haired miniature horse with his nose in a feed bucket. He had yellow-tan hair and a thin, wispy, cream-colored mane. His tail seemed to be half gone, short and frayed and brittle. One of his ears seemed mangled.

"Well, hi," I said, leaning down over the top of the wall. "Who are you?"

I didn't expect a reply from him, but a nearby human heard me.

"That's Old Lester," a man said, approaching from the rear of the barn in beat-up work boots and jeans. He was very tall, and moved slowly and deliberately toward me. He spoke as slowly as he moved. "Sorry I didn't hear you come in. Just getting Warrior's feed mashed in the back there."

"That's okay," I said. "Hi."

"Can I help you?"

"Well," I began, unsure of how to explain the visit. I took a deep breath and just plunged in from the beginning. "My name's April Helmbach, and I live in Plattsburgh. I heard about horse therapy the other day for the first time and was curious about how it all works. I mean, how you get your horses and your people."

The man put down the bucket he was hauling and stuck out his hand toward me. "Nice to meet you, April. I'm Daniel Farnsworth and my wife's Emma. We run this place."

"Oh, I saw your names when I was checking out the website last night," I said. "I thought I had read about every single one of the horses, but I must have missed this one."

Daniel chuckled, and we both stood over the rail

looking at the miniature horse feeding below. "Yeah, Lester's been around the block a couple of times," he said. "Petting zoos, pony carts, you name it. We think he got his tail and ear chewed off when he worked in a circus way back when. Chewed or frozen from exposure. He's a geezer now, though, so we only use him when we really need him."

"Wow," I said. "But how does this all work? I mean, what exactly do you do?"

"If you can keep me company, I can tell you," Daniel said. "But how'd you get here? Your mom, your dad—they wanna come in, too, and have a look around?"

"Actually, it's my aunt I live with, but thanks, she's not so into horses. Is that someone's breakfast?" I asked, indicating the bucket.

"This is for Warrior," Daniel said as I followed him toward another one of the sunken stalls. "Excuse me just a sec." Daniel disappeared into the back of the barn and reappeared from the outside, where he could get into the stall at grass level. I walked up to the stall and saw a huge bay gelding backed up into one of the corners. His back sagged like a bowl, and his head hung sleepily. In general, I couldn't believe how calm and quiet this barn was. You would never even have known there were any animals inside. It could not have more different from the McCann barn, where creatures were constantly making noises, as if to impose their opinions with nickers, neighs, honks, clucks, and snorts.

"We have no idea how old this guy is," Daniel said, patting Warrior's side as he placed the bucket in its slot. "Way more than thirty is all we know. Every day's a gift for him and us, 'cause he's great with our clients. When we got him he was starving to death, had no teeth, and couldn't eat a bite of food without choking or throwing up."

"No teeth?" I asked, amazed. "None, as in zero?"

"Zero," Daniel said. "We mash his oats and alfalfa into a pulp that he can get down safely. Just like baby food. And we add vitamins and everything else, all of it mashed."

I noticed that Warrior didn't rush right over and start gobbling, like Rainy Day did when I fed him. He just stood there listening.

"Yup," Daniel went on. "This horse has seen just about everything a horse can see."

"Like..."

"Well, first of all, he was a rodeo horse. A barrel racer. A roper. Then he did farmwork and probably took riders as a lesson horse, too. We don't know everything, of course."

Looking at the animal now, it was hard to imagine Warrior as active and young. I drifted over to a big wall on one end of the open space where yellowing newspaper articles about horse therapy were pinned to corkboard. I read a couple of these articles and couldn't believe how they had helped so many different kinds of people. There were snapshots of what I assumed were Willow Grove clients—smiling young kids in helmets slumped and tipped way over in the saddle, with teenagers and adults holding them steady.

"Exactly how does this all work?" I asked Daniel when he had returned from outside.

"Well, it's complicated," he began. "Different problems are addressed by different aspects of riding and different qualities of the horse. Some activities improve some problems; other movements improve other problems."

When he saw I was staring blankly, Daniel explained that the walking motion of the horse stimulates all the muscles and nerves in a nonwalking person's stomach. "Say you're in a wheelchair," he said. "When I put you on a horse and he starts to walk, the muscles in your belly are activated just as if you were doing the walking yourself. They get stronger, so you can sit up straighter in your chair, and your muscle tone will improve."

"I get it," I said.

"But there are other things, too," he said. "Less physical results. For a kid with severe emotional and neurological problems, just being around the horses—smelling them, touching them, listening to the sounds they make—helps the kids grow comfortable with unfamiliar situations in other environments."

I thought about Matt and the way he seemed to be managing the unfamliar environment of school.

"Our horses are sensitive to these kids," Daniel said, "but they don't freak out. They can't freak out."

"How can you be sure they won't?" I asked, thinking about all the horse-related freak-outs I knew all too well— the one that killed my parents, the one that made JP flee, the one where Rainy Day refused to budge no matter what I did.

"It's a matter of finding the right ones," Daniel said. "We take calm ones to begin with, we prescreen them to make sure they won't run, rear, kick, or bite. They cannot do anything at all, no matter what happens around them. And some of our clients do some pretty unpredictable things."

"Like what?"

"Like screaming for joy. Like walloping the horse to

show affection. Or like swatting at a fly and missing and hitting the horse by mistake. Some can't control their limbs at all, which can give the horse confusing directions. Our horses are trained and expected to withstand anything and everything in the way of sound, touch, and smell."

As if on cue, I heard a bloodcurdling cry from the direction of where we had left our car. I whipped around to see what could have made such a sound and saw only a smiling man carrying a small kid slung over his shoulder.

"Excuse me, April, for just a second," Daniel said. "I gotta say hi to my buddy Harry here."

It turned out that Harry was the little boy, and that the ear-piercing shriek was his way of saying how excited he was to go horseback riding. Not a single horse in the whole barn made a sound. I couldn't believe it. The only movement came from a barn swallow, who swooped from his nest in the rafters and zoomed outside. As I stood watching, a couple of women arrived for Harry's lesson. They wore matching T-shirts. A girl who looked about my age came in, too. It turned out she was a volunteer, one of the people who made sure the clients don't fall off. They also keep the horses steady. Although it depended on their needs, each rider basically had three people around at all times—one leading the horse, and two on each side. While

Daniel and his staff welcomed the first clients of the day, I went outside to check in with Aunt Patti. I found her sitting in the shade reading a book. She looked up as I approached and smiled.

"Well, what's it like?"

"Amazing," I said. "Are you okay out here? I wanted to ask Daniel a couple more questions but he got busy."

"Take your time, babe. It's lovely here."

Back in the barn, volunteers and staff were setting up the clients on their horses. In addition to Warrior, I saw an old dapple-gray and a pinto. One of the clients was a really little girl who wore thick glasses. Her hands were folded forward at an odd angle, and her fingers were bent at every knuckle. Still, she knew to lay her hands onto the saddle in front of her as the instructor encouraged. In a quiet parade, the riders, horses, and support staff walked slowly out of the barn and into the sunshine.

"Sorry for the interruption," Daniel said, returning to where I stood talking to the miniature horse, Lester. "On weekends we go from pretty dead to all systems go in a flash. I should have warned you."

"Oh, that's okay," I said. "I was just wondering, though. Do you have any clients with Asperger's?"

"Autistic kids, you mean? Sure we do. For some of

them, it's a matter of putting them in a situation with another living being where they don't feel socially awkward. A horse doesn't care if you're good with people or not. A horse, like any animal, accepts you for who you are. Some of those kids go on to learn so many facts about horses, they blow my mind. Why don't we step outside so you can take a look at how the lessons go?"

"Who rides Lester?" I asked as Daniel led me from the barn.

Daniel laughed. "Well, we let old Lester mind his own business, usually. But every so often we get a client who can't sit in a saddle no matter what. Then we harness Lester to a cart and let the child get pulled along behind him. They get a kick out of that."

We stood by the rail of the riding ring and watched the riding sessions.

"You know," I said finally, "I think my horse would be amazing at this."

I told Daniel about Rainy Day, his brush with death on the highway, the way he had stayed so calm throughout the floods of May, and how he always seemed to know exactly how I felt. "Instead of making him spook easily," I said, "all his trauma seems to have left him totally calm, especially when I'm around. Just about the only unexpected thing

Rainy Day ever does is sneeze."

"Sounds like he trusts you," Daniel said. "Trust is the only thing that can override their natural tendency to panic."

"Do you think Rainy Day could ever work here?" I asked as Aunt Patti walked over, tapping her watch with one finger to show me it was time to get going. She came up beside me.

"April?"

"I know," I said. "I'm almost ready. Daniel, this is my aunt, Patti Helmbach. Patti, this is Daniel Farnsworth."

They both said hi.

"Sounds like your niece here has got a nice gentle horse at home."

"She does," Aunt Patti said. I could hear that note of suspicion in her voice, the way she always sounded when she was afraid I was going to take on something bigger or more complicated than she was prepared to deal with. I had heard it back when I first asked to adopt Rainy Day. I was braced for her objection before I even brought up the request.

"I was just asking Daniel whether he thought Rainy Day might be able to work here," I said. "He'd be so great with these kids. And you know I've been worried about him getting bored."

We all watched as one of the little riders flung an arm up in the air with glee and lost her balance. The counselor on her right caught her and pushed her back into the center of the saddle. The horse she was riding didn't break stride at all.

"Well, I don't want to jump the gun here," Daniel said. "Or raise your hopes, April. My wife and I would have to come out and meet your guy. You can see for yourself what kind of nerves he has to have. We'd have to assess his gentleness. But that's all assuming it's okay with your aunt."

As I had so many times in the last few months, I felt like I was watching the inside of Aunt Patti's mind tick and whirl like factory machinery. She was probably weighing the possible benefits against the total inconvenience.

"I don't know," she said. "You've got an amazing situation here, but it's a pretty far drive. I don't know any of the details or the logistics."

"Now, I don't want to bias you," Daniel said. "But we've got another little piece of land out by Union, ten minutes or so outside of Plattburgh. We keep a couple of our horses out there for therapy, too. I mostly run this stable, and my wife runs that one."

"Oh, yeah, I think I saw that other place listed on your website," I suddenly remembered. "I thought it was a mailing address or something."

I was beaming inside but kept quiet. Chipping away at the inconvenience was an excellent strategy. After a few more back-and-forths, Aunt Patti and Daniel agreed that he and his wife should come out next weekend and screen Rainy Day for volunteering as a therapy horse. If he wasn't fit, then the whole plan would be moot. If he was fit, we'd figure out what to do at that point. I knew I might be pushing my luck to ask my next question, but I couldn't resist.

"Daniel, let's say I was interested in volunteering as an assistant here, how would I go about it?"

"Well," he said. "First off, you'd have to be fourteen. We've got the horses, but you would have to be trained. The volunteers have to learn how to put the safety of the client first at all times. That's about it. But you'll have to excuse me now, I've got a few things to take care of before this lesson's over."

We all shook hands, and Aunt Patti and Daniel agreed to talk on the phone to set up his screening visit. I was so excited walking back to the car, I could hardly stand it. Aunt Patti seemed cheerful, too, which I was relieved about. She and I sang along with the radio as we drove the rest of the way into St. Louis. First we stopped off at the botanical garden, where Aunt Patti needed to pick up some seedlings. Then we went to my grandma's for lunch. All my cousins, aunts, and uncles were there, and my grandma sat me down so she could hear "every last little thing about the summer and about the start of school." I filled her in as best I could, leaving out the fact that I suspected I had a crush on a boy with Asperger's. It was news to me, too.

Chapter

8

I was the second oldest of the cousins, so I spent the afternoon pushing the younger kids on the swings and pretending not to know where they were during hide-and-seek so they could feel like they were really tricking me. I also let myself lose at checkers four times in a row. But the whole time, I was distracted by thoughts about Matt. In my imagination I kept seeing his nice smile and his tousled hair. In my opinion, the totally disheveled look he had going made him more, not less cute. I wanted so badly to just sit down and talk with him alone, but I was also afraid. When he did manage to look me in the eye, his expression was so sincere and open, it was different from any boy I had ever known. Remembering his comment about *Into Thin Air,* how he had no idea how those people would have felt, I couldn't be sure whether he would or could like me back. And since I had never really *like-liked* anyone before, I didn't know what to expect from a so-called normal relationship, let alone one with someone who was different from anyone I had ever known. What was I supposed to do now?

Around four-thirty Aunt Patti and I got in the car to head back to Plattsburgh. We would drop everything off at home—mostly the plants Aunt Patti had bought—and then go over to Nelson's for an early dinner. As soon as we got home, I ran out to say hi to Rainy Day. He was as close to the fence as possible on the side of the yard nearest Lowell's house, nodding his head up and down. Lowell was blasting some hip-hop from his back porch and skipping rope on his driveway. I burst out laughing, because it seemed like Rainy Day was keeping time to the beat.

"You funny horse," I said. "Look what happens when I turn my back."

"Hey," Lowell said, seeing me come over to lead Rainy Day into the barn for the night.

"Hi."

"I called you earlier," Lowell said. His face was pink from exertion and his hair lay matted on his forehead. "You wanna watch a movie tonight?"

"Thanks, but I can't. We're going to Nelson's, and I still have homework. Sorry."

"No problem."

It was the kind of exchange Lowell and I had had nine thousand times before at least, but for some reason, this time he sounded genuinely disappointed. I did a double take, but he had already turned to go back to his house. I clucked Rainy Day to follow me, and set about his grooming more thoughtfully than usual.

Nelson and Shawn were whooping it up when we arrived for dinner. On the front porch, Shawn was in his wheelchair giggling, and Nelson was tipped all the way back in his dad's ancient rocker, wiping tears of laughter from his eyes. Aunt Patti was carrying a half-full baked bean casserole in her arms—part one of our leftovers. I cradled part two, which was a big bowl of fruit salad. Buster, Nelson's dog who had belonged to old Mr. McCann, sniffed around our legs and wagged his tail.

"Hey, Patti," Shawn said, recovering himself. "Hey, April."

"Hi, Shawn," I said. "Great to see you! Lemme put this stuff down and I'll come right out. Buster, quit sniffing at Chase's smell and let me get by."

Nelson jumped up and held open the screen door for us to pass through. "Thanks, you guys," he said. "You can set those in the kitchen. I just started the fire for the steaks."

Aunt Patti and I put down our loads and went back to the porch.

"So what's so funny," Aunt Patti said, leaning down to kiss Nelson hello.

"Oh, it's stupid," Nelson said. "Not worth repeating."

Shawn snickered, but didn't say anything. I sat down on the top step and scratched Buster behind the ears.

"So, Shawn," Aunt Patti said. "Catch us up. How are things?"

"Things are excellent," Shawn said. "But of course, the last time I saw you, they couldn't really have been worse."

We all laughed because that was such a Shawn thing to say. Back in May, he was living in a trailer, applying to college, and, after the floods, temporarily homeless. He had been an able-bodied guy, but he came back from two years in Iraq in a wheelchair and with no idea what to do. The first time I met him was in the library, when he was studying for college entrance exams. Now he had a sparkle in his eye and every little thing seemed to amuse him, especially Nelson.

"Tell April and Patti where you're headed," Nelson urged.

"Come January, I'll be at the University of Missouri in Rolla," he said. "They let me into their engineering school. Seems I picked up a thing or two about wires and fire overseas. At the ripe old age of twenty-two, I'm gonna learn to build things."

"That's great, Shawn," Patti said. "I'm serious."

"Yeah," I joined in. "I can just picture you designing bridges and whatever."

"In the meantime, though, between now and January, he's going to help me out—since I've been abandoned by my summer staff," Nelson said, meaning me and Lowell.

"Which means the first thing I'm going to engineer will be ramps up to this porch and into the barn," Shawn said. Now that the sun was down, he twisted his baseball cap around so that the bill was facing backwards. I noticed again how strong his arms were from pushing himself around. It was like Shawn had two different bodies—a big muscle-bound one from the waist up, and a thin, weak one from the waist down.

"I better go throw on those steaks," Nelson said.

"I'll keep you company," Aunt Patti said, following him down the stairs and around to the back of the house to the grill.

"Your new wheelchair's cool," I remarked, taking Nelson's place in the rocker.

"Yeah, it's kind of an ATV, an all-terrain type deal," Shawn said.

"So..." I said.

"So?"

"So, I was just wondering if you've ever heard of equine therapy."

"You mean equine as in horseback riding?" Shawn asked, leaning forward to dig a potato chip into a bowl of sour cream dip. I noticed he had to strain himself to get back up straight. "Nope, can't say as I have."

I took a deep breath. "It's this cool thing where people ride on horses to improve their various conditions, whatever they may be."

Shawn laughed. He and I always joked about things, and I was relieved that this was going to be no exception.

"April, are you implying that I have a condition? Since when is having two useless limbs a condition?"

"Now, now, Shawn," I scolded sarcastically, "don't turn bitter vet on me. Aunt Patti and I were at this place today, and met this guy who explained that riding on horseback makes your stomach do everything it would be doing as if you were walking yourself. It strengthens your torso. It also improves your balance."

I hoped Shawn would get hooked by the thought of being stronger. His not making a crack right away told me that he was interested.

"What are you driving at?" he finally said, after munching through another two potato chips. In the long pause, I heard Hannah nickering in the far field. JP must have wandered a little too far away.

"How about we put you on Rainy Day and you learn to ride?" I said.

"Me? Ride? The last time I was on horseback, as you may recall, I was hanging on for dear life while water swirled around my rib cage."

"Of course I *recall* that," I said, matching his facetious tone. "Just like I *recall* the extremely imaginative phrases you put together to express your compromised position. But I also remember that you stayed put right behind me. Come on, Shawn. Please? I'll be right there next to you. I need to practice with *someone*!"

"Oh, ho!" Shawn said. "So now we get to the point. You need a guinea pig."

I punched him on the shoulder. Just then Aunt Patti came back around to the front, carrying the platter of sizzling-hot steaks. The meat smelled delicious.

"Who's a guinea pig for what?" she said. "Dinner's ready. Come in and tell us."

Over dinner I explained what I thought was my brilliant plan. I would do equine therapy with Shawn in order to see how Rainy Day would do as a therapy horse and help Shawn build up his core strength. A person couldn't be too strong, I argued, when he said he was perfectly satisfied with his core strength as it was.

"April," Aunt Patti said, "I can't tell whether you're serious or not. But if you are, you need to wait until Daniel comes out to screen Rainy Day. You don't want to put Shawn in a dangerous position. You don't have the foggiest idea how this all works."

I hated it when Aunt Patti suddenly sounded like a scolding TV mom. Especially when she did it around other people.

"But that's just it," I said. "I can learn."

"I'm agreeing with you," Aunt Patti said. "I'm just saying learn first."

Nelson changed the subject to goats, which I was grateful for. Shawn offered to help design and construct the new pens.

"I just can't decide whether to raise them strictly for dairy or to have a flock bred for meat, too," Nelson said. "More and more people are into goat around here. I think I could muster a pretty lucrative business either way."

Patty mentioned her contacts with an old friend who already sold to the St. Louis farmers' market.

"Also, I've been doing a little research of my own," she said.

"Do tell," Nelson said playfully.

"Well, I'm thinking of getting into beekeeping," she said.

I knew Aunt Patti loved pollinators. She had produced a couple of scrapbooks about the various insects and birds that agriculture depended on. And she could go on and on about the butterflies, hummingbirds, and honeybees that hovered in her garden all through the growing season. "Sorry, April," she would say when I looked bored after fifteen-minute a lecture about pollen spores. "It's just the wannabe biology teacher in me coming out. I'll shut up." Then I would feel a little sorry for her, since I knew that I was the reason she had put off going to graduate school and becoming a teacher.

Shawn and Nelson both looked interested.

"You mean like making your own honey?" Shawn said.

"More like managing beehives so that the bees can make their own honey, with extra for us," Aunt Patti said, making herself clear as always. "And maybe even enough extra to sell."

Nelson looked over-the-top excited. "And I hope you guys realize that what with the spread of CCD, this is a superimportant time for small farmers to get into beekeeping."

"CCD?" Shawn repeated. "Sounds like an army acronym—Command and Cooperate with Discipline."

"Colony Collapse Disorder," Nelson explained. "It's a mysterious ailment that's causing honeybee hives to die off. The bees fly off in the morning to collect pollen but don't come back."

"Sounds like they go AWOL," Shawn said. "Which really *is* an army term—Away Without Leave."

Nelson ignored Shawn this time and gazed at Patti with absolute adoration. It was a look out of a romance movie—a couple of nerdy lovebirds way into insects.

"Cool," I said to Aunt Patti. "So between you and Nelson, you'd have vegetables, goat cheese, goat milk, and honey."

"That's the idea," she said.

I was beginning to get the idea behind the plan: Aunt Patti and Nelson were cooking up a future together.

After dinner I went out to the barn and grabbed two lead ropes off a hook. I found JP with Hannah in the shade, tearing up fresh long grass. JP shook his mane when he saw me and dashed ten yards away.

"Hey, boy," I said, laughing. "I'm not going to make

you do any work right now. It's time for dinner and bed. Come on."

JP threw his head back and ran a little farther. Then he turned to face me, planting his hooves firmly in the soft field.

"Suit yourself," I said. "I'll get your mom first."

I hooked Hannah's lead rope under her halter, patted her strong neck, and walked her over to JP. Hannah was a large brown bay, an older mare who knew the routines of daily life. At only a couple of months, JP was still checking to see if there were exceptions to the everyday rules. He watched Hannah and me walking over, and I could tell he was trying to decide whether it was worth a fight. Luckily, JP made the right choice. Without hesitating, I snapped on his lead and got between the two horses, the one big and slow, the other small and energetic.

Once the two horses were settled in their stall for the night, I went back and told Aunt Patti that I was ready to go home. Shawn said he'd better get going, too, and we watched as he rolled himself over to his pickup, an old white Jeep with large rust patches on the hood and doors. He had had the truck retrofitted to be accessible so that he could get in and drive on his own. He climbed into the driver's seat, collapsed his chair, then pulled it up and slung it into the truck bed behind him. He shot us a big grin and pulled away.

"I'm happy this worked out for you and Shawn," Aunt Patti said to Nelson as he walked us to our own truck. We were both carrying the clean and empty casserole and bowl that we had brought from Grandma's house.

"Yeah," Nelson said. "It's great for both of us."

Aunt Patti put the empty casserole in the middle of the seat and turned back to Nelson.

"See you, babe," she said as they clasped each other around the waist and kissed goodbye. It was still a little weird for me to see Aunt Patti getting physical with someone in that kind of way. Weird, but also nice. It made her seem even younger.

"Thanks for dinner, Nelson," I said, slamming my door shut. He gave me a hasty pat on the shoulder.

By now it was dark, and we drove home through the shadows of the overhanging oaks and cedars that lined the road from the McCann place back to Plattsburgh. At first we rode in silence, but then Aunt Patti broke it.

"I'm sorry about not being so enthusiastic about the Shawn thing, April," she said. "When I see how capable he is of taking care of himself, I realize he's not going to let you put him in a situation he can't get out of if he wants to."

"Thanks," I said. "But I'm not going to have any time before next week anyway. I was just mad that you said it in front of everyone."

"I know. I'm sorry."

"That's okay," I said, only half attentively. I was already thinking about the next day, and Matt, and Lowell's unusual disappointment earlier, and whether the athletic director would let me substitute horse-related work for a sport. Being back at school was like swimming in the ocean. You had to be ready for one wave after another.

Chapter

It was one wave after another that second week of school. On Monday morning Lowell cornered me to see if I knew anything about some scandal involving the budget for the math club. As a reporter for the school paper, he was trying to dig up facts on whether the math club advisor had allowed the club to use money to buy some software that wasn't allowed.

Later that day I sat with Matt at lunch and tried to talk to him to see how things were going. At first he seemed relaxed, and we talked a long time about the Wizard tournament he had played in on Sunday. He had beaten this other kid with a special deck he had created that nobody had ever beaten. Even though I don't know anything about Wizard, I was totally happy just looking at him and thinking how adorable he was when he wasn't worried. But then a couple of my friends sat down with us and he got flustered. It was like he suddenly didn't know what to do with himself. He stopped talking and ate the rest of his lunch mechanically. At the bell he leaped up and ran away.

On Tuesday, I finally went in to see the athletic director about my sports requirement. Mr. Bennock's desk was covered with schedules, announcements, and fliers. In the corner behind him leaned a teepee of field hockey sticks, and in the other corner was a shoebox filled with the tiny spikes kids screwed into the bottom of their cross-country running shoes. On every wall were the framed pennants, awards, and prizes won by all our school teams over the years. Mr. Bennock sat forward in his chair and told me to explain my request.

"You see, Mr. Bennock," I said, "it all started when I adopted this horse at the end of last year."

I explained what caring for Rainy Day required. "It's not just grooming," I said. "It's riding and training him. And I'm also mostly responsible for training a foal that was born early in the summer and for looking after his dam. Plus now—and this is the really P.E. part—I'm thinking of volunteering at a stable where horses are used to do therapy with kids who have various disabilities."

"All right, I'm with you so far. Go on and tell me a little more about that," he said, cradling in one hand a baseball paperweight made of solid glass.

By the end of the meeting, Mr. Bennock said that he would sign off on my A.A.P.—an alternative athletic program—if Rainy Day and I got the job at Willow Grove.

"Thank you so much, Mr. Bennock," I said, walking out. Getting that permission was a huge relief.

But then on Thursday afternoon, another wave came along that really knocked me off balance. It was an overcast afternoon and I was in the barn with Rainy Day around five o'clock, sitting at my desk doing my homework. Rainy Day was standing in his stall eating from a bucket of oats, when I heard someone call my name.

"April?"

I went out and saw Lowell on my back porch. He thought I was in the house.

"Hi! You done with practice already?" I said.

"Coach made it short," he said. "We have a meet tomorrow and he wants us rested."

"Oh."

I wasn't sure what to say. Normally Lowell and I just called each other or walked into each other's houses without any advance notice.

"So what's up? I'm just doing homework out here to keep Rainy Day company," I said, staying by the barn door.

"I'm just wondering . . . " he began. And then I got that peculiar feeling again, the one I had had when he mentioned the movie on Sunday. Lowell was acting different. There was something phony about the way he was being with me. I had a feeling I knew what it was, but I didn't want it to be what I thought.

Don't ask me out, please don't ask me out.

Because Lowell and I were good friends, I really didn't want to hurt his feelings by telling him I didn't want to go out with him. I liked things exactly the way they were. And also, that I happened to like someone else, who was probably unlikely to ever like me back.

"About the eighth-grade dance," he said nervously.

All my nerves were on edge by now, which may be one reason that we were saved from total awkwardness by... Rainy Day!

An ear-piercing neigh came from inside the small barn. Lowell dashed over and we both ran inside to see what could have made him call out like that.

"What is it, boy?" I said, then laughed as I realized that he had kicked over his feed bucket and spilled all the oats on the floor by his front hooves, where they were now hidden below the clean hay at his feet.

"Such commotion for that?" I joked, slapping him gently on the flank. Rainy Day looked at me with one eye. I picked up the bucket and replaced it on the rack. Then I scooped in another portion. I turned and saw Lowell sitting at my desk chair watching me. But he must have lost his nerve, because what he finally asked was something he had said a thousand times before.

"Hey, can I eat at your place tonight? My mom and dad are out."

"Sure. I think we're having enchiladas. In fact, I think I'm the one who's supposed to put them in the oven now. Aunt Patti left a note."

"Anything would be great," Lowell said. "What's there to eat now? I'm starved. And I could strangle Finnegan for making that lab report due tomorrow."

I heaved a sigh of relief. Nothing could have sounded more normal.

I was so excited for Saturday morning, I could hardly sleep the night before. Daniel and Emma had confirmed that they would be arriving around nine, so I made sure that Rainy Day was up, fed, groomed, and turned out by eight-thirty. When their big dusty pickup pulled up, we were ready. Chase ran full speed over to greet the newcomers before I commanded him back to the porch. Even though Rainy Day was completely used to having a dog around, I figured the last thing he needed was an extra distraction.

"So, this is our man," Daniel said, coming slowly toward Rainy Day to greet him. He had a clipboard tucked under one arm for taking notes, and a stubby pencil behind his ear. Daniel opened his free hand under Rainy Day's muzzle so he could collect the new scent. Rainy Day flicked his ears forward and his eyes were bright.

At the sound of the passenger door slamming, we all turned to watch Emma approach. Equally tall but much slimmer than her broad husband, she had a birdlike face and streaked blond hair cut in a short layered style. Set in a suntanned and wrinkled face, her bright blue eyes seemed energetic and young in a way that matched her blue jeans and white T-shirt. She was so tall and lean, she reminded me of a giraffe. Emma came right over to let Rainy Day have a long look at her.

"You sure look like a sweet horse," she said, rubbing his head and ears. "I'm sorry we're going to have to do stuff you may not like." Emma turned to her husband. "Did you tell April what's going to happen now?"

"I thought I'd introduce you first," Daniel said, kidding her.

"Sorry," Emma said to me. "I always meet the horse and assume I already know the person. I'm Emma Farnsworth." She smiled and raised her hand for me to shake.

"I'm April. My aunt said she'd be out in a little bit. She's still getting dressed."

"That's fine," Daniel said, watching every single movement Rainy Day made in response to our voices. "April, why don't you lead him over to the middle of the paddock? We'll start off with you close by, then assess him without you there keeping him comfortable. Emma, go on and bring over the blue thing."

"The blue thing?" I repeated quietly, wondering what that might be.

I walked Rainy Day to the spot Daniel had indicated. Out of the corner of my eye, I saw Emma jog in long strides over to the truck and haul out a large blue plastic container, the kind of box used for packing food on camping trips. It was about two and a half feet wide, a foot and a half deep, and two feet across. She returned and set it down in the grass nearby.

"Okay," Daniel said. "So here's what's gonna happen. You stand there holding him just the way you are, April. I'm going to walk around him, touch him, talk to him, and even whisper in his ear. I'm going to touch his legs, his feet, and then I'm going to do a bunch of potentially agitating things around his flank and sides in general."

"His sides? Why there?" I asked.

"Say you're a horse in the wild," Emma said as Daniel bent one of Rainy Day's ears forward and backward. "You're standing around grazing with the others, but you're sick, or old, or very young. When that cougar or wolf comes after you, he's going to go for your side first. If he can get a good chomp out of you there, it's a good bet you'll go down. Once you're off your feet, fleeing is less likely, and he's more likely to have himself a meal."

Rainy Day blew air out of his nostrils but otherwise stayed still. Daniel chuckled.

"Yeah," he said. "Horses will always protect their flanks. If they're going to be twitchy about anything, it'll happen if you come at them from here."

As he said this, he slapped Rainy Day pretty hard on his side. I inhaled sharply, silently hoping that Rainy Day would not flinch. His eyes shone, but he stood still as a statue. Emma and Daniel exchanged a look of approval.

"Does he give you any grief when you pick out his hooves, April? Or scrub his legs?"

"Nope," I said proudly. "Nothing I've ever done, grooming-wise, has ever set him off."

"So I guess we're ready for the box?" Emma said to Daniel, and he nodded.

She opened the two flaps of the blue camping box and

began to rummage inside. I leaned over to peek in and saw all kinds of colorful toys, playthings, household tools, and gadgets. There were Mardi Gras beads, pool noodles, balloons, fly swatters, a hula hoop, and a manual eggbeater. I saw a yellow plastic squeaky duck and a couple of party blowers. Emma stuck one of the party blowers in her mouth and grabbed the duck. At the sparkly rustle of the streamers, Chase came bounding over from the porch, where he had been curled up, watching us from a distance. He barked at the streamers.

"No, Chase," I said firmly, pointing my arm back at the porch. "Go lie down. None of this is for you."

He gave one weak yap and walked briskly back to his sleeping pad, where he could keep an eye on things but stay out of trouble.

Emma walked right up to Rainy Day, showed him the duck, and squeaked it in each ear.

I couldn't believe my eyes. The things Emma and Daniel were doing would have driven me crazy, but Rainy Day showed no signs of being bothered. In fact, it sort of looked like he had a twinkle in his eye, as if saying, *I've seen people do some crazy things in my life, but this takes the cake.*

Still, I was worried that eventually they would go too far and make him react in some bad way.

Next Emma stepped into the blind spot behind him and cranked the eggbeater so that it whirred like a throng of insects. Nothing. No reaction.

"Okay, honey," Daniel said, marking notes on his clipboard. "Phase two."

Emma put a hand on my shoulder. "April, can you get Rainy Day saddled for us? This next part we do while I'm riding him."

"Sure," I said, leading Rainy Day to the barn and hooking his lead rope to the hitching post. I swung on the blanket, the saddle, and started buckling the old leather girth, which I noticed again was showing the cracks of age.

"You're doing amazing, buddy," I said. "Just keep it up."

We walked back to the center of the paddock.

"So, April, now we're going to ask you to go have a seat for a little while. Emma's going to ride him, if that's okay. You're going to see us try our best to annoy the heck out of him, but we're only doing it because that's what some of the kids do, and we want to know if he'll react."

Now I was on pins and needles myself. Before walking away I went over and whispered in his ear.

"It's all okay, boy," I said. "This is just a test, and you have nothing to worry about. Just stay calm and know I'm right over there watching."

I kissed the side of his face and headed over to the porch to sit with Chase.

Daniel wasn't kidding when he said they would try to get him to react. Emma walked him slowly around the paddock while Daniel kept up by her side making notes every few minutes. She bopped him on the head with a pool noodle. Daniel rattled beads in each ear. Emma blew up a balloon and popped it behind his head. Daniel popped another one right in his face. At one point I buried my head in Chase's fur.

"I can't watch, this is too disturbing," I said, then looked up right away so as not to miss a single test.

Emma walked him over to the driveway and stood him stock-still facing their truck. Daniel climbed in, started the car, and revved the engine loudly. Rainy Day stared ahead as if it were just another fun day in Plattsburgh, Missouri. Then Daniel really gunned the engine, causing a couple of cardinals to fly off the electric wire that ran beside our house.

In that moment, I remembered a scene out of *Black Beauty*, which I had read early in the summer. In that classic old horse story, Black Beauty's wise owner sent him to a neighboring farm that bordered on some railroad tracks. There were cows and sheep sharing the same meadow as

Black Beauty, and when the first train went screeching by, Black Beauty freaked out and galloped as far as he could from the tracks. But when he saw that the sheep and cows hardly blinked at the passing train, and noticed that all the other trains that went by never left the tracks to come into the field, he eventually got used to them and lost all his fear. I realized then that Rainy Day's experiences in life had taught him a similar lesson. Scary things can happen— loud, annoying, and physical—but if you see others around you who are paying no attention to those things, you gain confidence that you will be all right, too. I couldn't think of any other reason why nothing Emma and Daniel did were making him react. Rainy Day, who had lived through a horrible accident, wild thunderstorms, a flood, and all the rest, was the very model of gentleness.

"What's going on out here?" Aunt Patti said as she came out to the porch and saw Rainy Day being trotted around while a bright yellow scarf was dangled over his eyes.

"It looks insane, doesn't it?" I said. "But he's been amazing so far. I think he's going to get the job."

She took a noisy slurp of coffee.

"Well," she said, "I don't think it's a job I could do, that's for sure. It's hard enough trying not to annoy a teenager. I don't think I could ever try so hard to bother a horse on purpose."

After a half hour more, Emma and Daniel brought Rainy Day up to the fence and called me over. They patted him all over and told him how great he had done, that they had only seen two or three other horses so calm and gentle in their lives. I felt so proud as I removed his saddle, his blanket, and his bridle. Threading on his halter, I gave him a kiss on the nose and sent him off to graze. Before walking away, he nuzzled me under my arm. In my back pocket I found an alfalfa cube and snuck it to him before he trotted away happily.

"Usually, even with the calm ones," Daniel said, watching Rainy Day admiringly, "we get to a point that they can't take it but we feel okay about it. This horse never even seemed to get to that point."

"Yeah," Emma said. "We called it off because there's nothing left we could think up to do. This guy is unflappable. He'll be great with our kids."

"But what about me?" I asked. "How do you screen me?"

Emma put her hand on my shoulder. "Why don't you come back and see us one afternoon this week? You can watch a lesson up close and learn what you need to know that way. Given how gentle Rainy Day is, you might not be aware of the warning signs a spooked horse will show."

"You may be right," I said, concerned. "The only time Rainy Day balked was one time when I tried to lead him someplace he knew better than to go. And even then, he just sort of reared up out of the blue, and I slid off behind him."

"Exactly," Emma said. "But I'm sure there were signs in the moments before that happened."

Daniel looked up from loading all the toys back into their blue box. "I totally agree," he said. "But anticipating those moments is mostly using your head and common sense. The number one rule in our situation is that the safety of the child or rider always comes before the horse. But there's only been one time we had a volunteer lose sight of that."

"What happened?" I asked. Daniel shook his head, as if he still couldn't believe it.

"It was late spring, the first nice warm day. The volunteer was walking along beside her rider, just like she was supposed to," Emma said. "Suddenly she looked down and saw a snake, just a little harmless garter snake warming himself in the grass. She freaked out and ran off, leaving the horse and kid alone. Luckily for us, the horse didn't spook and run, too. And Daniel was only ten or so steps away."

"I don't think I'd ever do anything like that," I said, by way of reassuring them.

Aunt Patti came over and offered them a cup of coffee or something else to drink, but Emma said they had to get going, that they had a couple of clients scheduled for lunchtime.

"So, Patti, assuming it's all right with you, we'll see April one day this week at your convenience?"

"You know," Aunt Patti said, "I'm afraid it will have to be next week at the earliest."

I must have looked stricken, but she looked at me and smiled. "Didn't you say you had to be fourteen to do this, babe?"

I had completely forgotten! I would have to wait until after my birthday on the eighteenth.

"Oh, well," Emma said, "that's not too far away. We'll be there when you're ready. In the meantime, assuming everything will work out, I'm going to plan on Rainy Day spending most of the fall weekends working, if that's okay. I think he'll enjoy the company of the other horses and the challenge of the experience."

"I do, too," I said.

"And at some point we'll decide if you and he want to keep it up," Daniel said.

"Sounds good," I said, and Aunt Patti nodded her agreement.

We watched them drive away, then wandered together over to the vegetable garden. The tomatoes and peppers were at the peak of their growing season. I reached down and plucked off a couple of cocktail tomatoes and popped them into my mouth. Warm from the sunshine, they were filled with juicy tomato flavor. I pulled off two more and ate them. Aunt Patti crouched down and yanked a couple of weeds that had sprouted around the butter lettuce.

"This will be really cool, April," she said. "I'm proud of you."

"Thanks. I think it'll be fun."

"But we still don't have a birthday plan for you, you know. Do you have any sense of what you want to do, or who you want to be with, friends-wise? Lowell? Ruby? Both? Neither?"

It was a lot easier when a birthday meant four girls and cake at the pottery place or my whole class at the bowling alley. How did I want to celebrate fourteen? And how could I have not figured this out before now?

Chapter

The patterns of tooling on each one of the western saddles were amazingly intricate. Different swirls, curlicues, flowers, and zigzags made each saddle unique. I looked closely at every one, imagining how they would look on Rainy Day. And these were just the saddles. In other parts of the tack shop were the bridles, halters, bits, blankets, and other things a horse needed. The shop, a big open area divided into sections by item, smelled of leather and sawdust. It was the afternoon of my birthday, and I was exactly where I wanted to be.

Earlier that morning, after waking me up with an off-key rendition of "Happy Birthday to You," Aunt Patti had made my special birthday breakfast, which she knew so well that I never even had to spell it out beforehand: French toast with whipped cream and preserves made from her homegrown strawberries, and bacon on the side. Over breakfast she handed me an envelope filled with cash. A lot of cash.

"Jeez," I said. I had never seen that much money in my life.

"This is what that bond I mentioned kicked off by way of a premium after ten years," she said. "The principle is going to stay put until it comes due, I think when you're twenty-one."

"And I can do anything at all with this?"

"As long as it's not totally wacko, sure." Aunt Patti laughed. "Your grandma's got a college fund growing for you under her watch, so this money doesn't have to be saved for that."

"Maybe I'll put some away for Rainy Day's care—feed and whatnot—and mess around with what's left," I said.

"Sounds like a plan," Aunt Patti said, reaching across the breakfast table and cupping my chin.

After tending to Rainy Day but before leaving for school, I stuck the envelope in my top bureau drawer under my socks. I met Lowell outside and he greeted me perfectly naturally, which was a huge relief.

"Hey, happy birthday, April."

"Thanks."

On the way to school we talked a little about his newspaper article, which was coming along. But then we fell quiet and swung into a matched rhythm of walking. The rest of the day was perfect. Matt accidentally brushed into me while rushing past my locker. He turned and smiled an apology, then later on sat with me at lunch. For a while it was just the two of us, and out of the blue he mentioned that he had "this condition" that he didn't really like to talk about. He seemed not to know that I might have suspected that there was anything unusual about him.

"I'm really socially awkward," he said. "But I can't understand how not to be. Awkward, I mean."

I decided to be direct.

"How does the dictionary help you? The one you carry around and use all the time."

"I like reading the words," he said. "I like going in order. I've gone through the whole dictionary five times so far. Today, just before assembly, I stopped in the middle of the D's at *dissimulate*."

"Which means . . . " I said encouragingly.

"To pretend," Matt replied. "It's what I do when I'm at school. Kind of. So that I seem like I fit in."

How sad, I thought. Here he was thinking he was fitting in, when the effort only made him seem more odd compared to regular kids. Matt's skin was pale and smooth. He had the faintest sign of a mustache on his upper lip. And his brown wavy hair fell in untended swoops across his forehead.

"I think it's cool that you can remember all those words," I said.

"Do you really think so?"

"I do," I said. "I really do."

All afternoon I thought about the smile he smiled just then above his chicken salad sandwich. It expressed relief, pleasure, and something like surprise. And it made my day.

After Aunt Patti dropped me off at the tack shop after school, I knew it was time to stop thinking about Matt and start thinking about what I wanted to buy for Rainy Day.

I stood before the racks of saddles and focused on choosing a color and a style. There were different shades of brown and black, and even some with silver or gold trim around the horn or down along both sides of the cantle. After saying good afternoon to me, the owner of the store went back to working behind the counter. He was a young guy in a cowboy hat, jeans, and boots. He seemed used to people spending long amounts of time thinking through their purchases. As he shuffled papers on the glass counter, he bobbed his head and shoulders rhythmically to the flowing, regular beat of a string quartet whose music came out of a beat-up, ancient-looking radio. It was funny, I thought, a rough cowboy dude listening to classical music. You never know about people, I guess.

Rainy Day was a bay, a perfect chestnut almost all over, except for a diamond on his forehead. A deep chocolate brown saddle would look fantastic on him, I thought. Right now his old saddle had gotten paler and bleached out by the sun, and was cracked all over from wear and tear. But nothing too ornate, I thought, passing by some of the fancier ones. I stopped for a long time in front of a smooth, glossy brown saddle, plain everywhere except for some delicate flowery swirls around the horn and along the bottom. The swirls looked like ivy, winding up and around the curves and bends of the leather. A pair of matching stirrups hung beside this saddle. I looked at other ones, too, but my eye always came back to the ivy set.

I moved along to the bridles, halters, and bits. These I actually took in my hands and manipulated, as if to see whether I would feel comfortable or not. I would be dealing with these items day in and day out. They would need to feel good in my hands. I found one bridle that looked especially cool. It had nice decorated connections at the places where two straps came together, and a sort of yellow woolly pad along the crown that looked like it would be super soft.

Finally I browsed among the quilted saddle pads and blankets. I loved the colorful Navajo patterns with the fringes. The soft wool seemed thicker and more protective than the ones we had inherited from my parents. I couldn't help but check out the latest, newest tools—the picks, brushes, currycombs, shampoos, and various gadgets for making tails and manes easier to care for and dress up. I messed around with a bunch of these, too. All of them seemed better than the stuff I had been using.

"Excuse me," I said to the guy at the counter.

"You about done there?" he asked good-naturedly, turning down his radio.

"I think so," I said. "It's hard to decide. Everything's gorgeous."

"It's all like this until it gets into a barn, now, ain't it?"

I laughed.

"Show me what you're thinkin' about," he said, climbing off his stool and coming around to my side of the counter. "But first off, how big's your horse? Gotta make sure you size the saddle and girth right."

I told him and was relieved to hear that the saddle I liked best would work.

The guy said his name was Greg, and he spent another half hour or so with me going over the care of the saddle, and how to break it in so as not to irritate Rainy Day.

"You got an unlimited budget?" he asked.

"Well, let's just say my budget is large enough to get what I want."

I didn't feel like explaining that my birthday wealth sprang from a gift my grandparents gave me when my parents died.

"That'll work," Greg said, flipping to a fresh page in his invoice book. Together we assembled all the items I had picked out and carried them into the open area by the front door. Just as we finished, Aunt Patti pushed through the door, ringing the little bell that swung along when it opened. Her eyes widened at the sight of all the equipment I had amassed.

"Isn't that an unbelievable saddle?" I blurted as soon as I saw her.

"It sure is."

"This is Greg," I said to her as she stood watching us deposit the last few things.

"Hey there," Greg said.

"Hi," Aunt Patti said.

"She's all paid up," Greg said. "I can help you load. What kinda car you got?"

"Oh, we've got a pickup," Aunt Patti said.

"That'll make things nice and easy," Greg said.

We carried everything to the back of the car and Greg

shook my hand. "You promise to come back now if anything doesn't work for you, okay?"

"I will. Thanks," I said.

Back home, I had just enough time to get Rainy Day decked out in his new tack for a short ride. I led him outside and tied him to the fence. He watched my every move back and forth from the truck, as if wondering what we were up to. He twitched the skin of his back as I threw on the new saddle pad, then relaxed briefly when he felt how soft the fresh quilting was. It took me longer to adjust the saddle and girth, because I had to figure out which hole to buckle everything on.

"Please stop that stamping and shifting, Rainy Day," I said. I sounded like Aunt Patti used to when I was young, when she would try to braid my hair and I wouldn't stand still. "This will go much faster if you cooperate, and you'll be more comfortable if this is tight enough."

Half complying, he stamped just one front foot and snorted. Then he stood still.

"There," I said, standing back to regard the final outfit as a whole. "Wow. You look amazing."

Rainy Day turned his head to look at me, then swished his tail. The deep brown leather glistened in the late afternoon sun. The bridle, the reins, the new bit—everything looked even better than I had imagined. I hadn't realized how shabby and worn our old tack was until seeing Rainy Day turned out in his new things.

"Now you can hang out with the popular crowd," I joked. "All you need is the latest cell phone."

"April?" Aunt Patti called out from the house. "We'll leave for dinner in about a half hour, okay?"

"Sounds good," I yelled back. We were going out with Nelson to my favorite restaurant, my birthday dinner place where I always ordered a shrimp cocktail and prime rib. But before getting changed, I still had time for a very short ride. The stirrups and reins felt stiff, and I could feel Rainy Day trying to get used to his new bit. While he adjusted, I gave him his head as much as possible. We rode around the paddock for ten minutes, and then I took everything off and gave him an extra scoop of oats, a hug around the neck, and a kiss on the nose.

"Happy birthday to me," I murmured.

Chapter

The next weekend we put Rainy Day into his trailer and drove over to the Willow Grove stable near Plattsburgh. Emma was going to train me to be a volunteer and give Rainy Day a little experience with actual clients. Aunt Patti kissed me good-bye and said she'd be back later in the afternoon, unless she heard from me to come sooner. We unhitched the trailer and she drove away.

It was gray and windy that Sunday morning. Dead brown leaves swirled around our feet as we walked toward the big open barn doors to meet Emma, who was waving us along. Rainy Day's mane flapped in the gusts.

"There's fall in the air this morning, isn't there?" she said to me as Rainy Day and I came up. A small sign on the barn door said: WILLOW GROVE WEST: EQUINE-ASSISTED THERAPY

"Yup," I said. "I just hope it doesn't rain."

Emma looked up. "I think we're okay. First thing we're going to do is hitch old Lester to the cart. Adrienne's coming at ten. She loves her 'horse and buggy,' as her dad says."

"What do I do with Rainy Day?"

"For now you can let him stand over there to get to know the other horses. Then we'll get his saddle on and see how you both do with one of our regular kids."

"Sounds good," I said.

Just like the other day at the St. Louis site, the horses in the barn were all quiet and still. A person would hardly know they were there. I helped Emma drag over the little red pony cart, and then she brought out the little miniature horse. I watched as she put on his tack and hitched him to the cart. He submitted with all the patience in the world.

"I can't get over how relaxed all these animals are," I said. "Do you move them back and forth from site to site every day?"

"Not that often. It depends on the schedule of sessions, and who's coming when. You'll see most of the same horses at both places, though."

Emma tugged at one of the buckles to make sure it was secure. The horse hardly budged. "Nope," Emma said, "you'll never see an old stallion here, or even a retired racer. No one with nerves!"

"They don't even flinch when the wind kicks up," I said, marveling at how Lester ignored the sudden bang of a shutter against the side of the barn.

"Nope. They don't. And as a volunteer here, you won't, either."

"I'll try," I said.

"If it helps, remember that a horse will naturally react like a mirror to whatever emotions are around it. They sense and reflect. It's a good bet that if you can keep yourself calm, he will, too."

Emma looked up as a car pulled into the gravel circle in front of the barn. She whispered to me hastily that this was probably Adrienne. Adrienne had a bone disease that made her incapable of walking, Emma said. Her leg bones were growing too quickly and hurting her hips and her knees. I nodded and waited for instructions. A man got out and opened up the backseat to carry out a small girl. Her legs and arms seemed very thin, but she had a big smile on her face. She looked like she was about eight years old. Emma beamed.

"Here's our girl," she said, going straight to the man and his daughter. "Lester's all ready for you."

"Where's that horse and buggy," the dad said. "There he is," turning so that Adrienne could see Lester standing patiently in the ring.

"This is April," Emma said, introducing me. "She's one of our new volunteers and she'll be leading Lester this morning. Dad, you help us get Adrienne situated in the cart and we'll be ready to go."

"Hi, Adrienne," I said.

"Hi," she answered shyly.

"April, please come and take hold of Lester for me," Emma said. "Now, the only thing you really have to remember is to stay right by his head here, move slowly, and start and stop as I say so. Adrienne's dad will be on one side of her, and I'll be on the other, so you don't have to worry about her. Only about Lester."

I gathered the lead rope in my hand and stood ready to walk. Compared to Rainy Day, Lester was tiny. He barely came up to my waist. I got a close-up look at his partial ear. A gooey bit of mucus or something lay in the corner of his brown eye, but I didn't have anything to wipe it away with.

Before settling his daughter into the cart, Adrienne's dad dipped her down so that she could pat Lester on the other side of his head and neck from where I stood. She giggled when he sneezed. Then Emma settled Adrienne into the cart seat. Her dad put a helmet on her head and strapped it under her chin. She leaned way back in the seat and had her legs stretched in front of her, I guess so that she wouldn't be uncomfortable. They put the reins into her hands, but I saw that they weren't attached to Lester, only to a hook in the cart.

"Okay, April, let's take a walk. To start off, we'll go around the ring once, and then maybe head off on the pony path for a few minutes if everything's going fine."

"Got it. Come on, Lester." I clucked. "Let's go, boy."

Lester put himself into motion at the slowest walk I ever saw. His short legs could only go so far. Plus he was old. It was actually hard for me to walk so slowly. I turned every so often to see the smile of ecstasy on Adrienne's face as she jiggled the reins up and down. The big wheels of the pony cart rolled slowly around and around. At first I thought I would go crazy moving so slowly, but after a few minutes I got the hang of what the lesson was all about—it had nothing to do with actually *getting* somewhere. The ride was designed for Adrienne's benefit—for her sake, the slower, the better. It gave her more time to relish the experience, and her giddy appreciation was contagious.

Forty-five minutes had gone by when we pulled back in front of the barn door. Adrienne's father lifted her out of the cart and chatted a while with Emma. Meanwhile, an older volunteer came up to me and introduced herself. She looked around nineteen or twenty, and wore a white T-shirt and jeans. A laminated name tag was clipped to the collar of her shirt.

"Hi, April. I'm Virginia. I'm supposed to set you up as a sidewalker now. You and Thunder are getting ready for David, who comes at eleven."

"A sidewalker?"

"Just what it sounds like," Virginia said. "You walk beside the stirrup on the left side and hold on to David's leg while he rides. You brace his calf and knee, so he doesn't tip over. I'll be on his other side, and another volunteer will be leading the horse. Is this your first day?"

"It is," I said.

"Pretty satisfying, isn't it? To see these kids so happy?"

"It's great," I said simply. At that point I couldn't quite explain to a total stranger what the experience had been like for me.

Thunder was a small brown-and-white pinto. He came up to my armpit and wore a saddle that had a handlebar across the front where the horn would have been on a normal western saddle. Virginia and I helped a mom lift her little boy, David, into the saddle. I guessed David to be around four years old. He had a tiny face and wore glasses. His huge helmet almost completely covered his head so you could only see his glasses and his big soft cheeks. Unlike some of the other kids I had seen, David looked very serious and concentrated, like a business executive trying out a new design for a car surrounded by the car's designers. It never even occurred to me to ask Virginia what was "wrong" with him. All I needed to do was hang on to his right leg and steady him if he lost his balance. Even on Thunder's, back. David's head was only a little higher than mine. He grasped the bar with two hands and looked straight ahead.

The volunteer at Thunder's head chatted a little to David as she led us into the ring.

"You hangin on there, buddy?"

David didn't reply, but Virginia did. "Oh, we're doing great back here, thanks. It's a nice day for riding."

Even though we were bracing David's legs, I could tell that his torso was working, just as Daniel had explained. His hips, stomach, and chest rocked forward and backward in the rhythm of Thunder's walking gait. Still, David looked serious. His gaze fell directly ahead and never wavered. I settled in for another twenty-five minute walk. Sometimes we all chatted, and other times we fell silent. Either way, David stayed all business. Until...

Thunder took a step and let out a long and loud blast of gas. At that, David turned to look at me in surprise, his huge blue eyes magnified behind his thick glasses. Then his face opened up and he started to laugh. He squealed and laughed so hard that he nearly fell against my shoulder.

"Hang on up there," I said. "Whoa. We gotta get this guy back upright."

"The old fart trick never fails," Virginia said. "Thunder knows it gets 'em every time."

A few days later I was at the McCann place after school, working with JP on the long line. We were in the riding ring, and JP was moving through his gaits pretty smoothly as I stood in the center of the ring holding one end of the rope. At one command, he went from a walk to a trot. At another, he sped up to a canter. It seemed to me he was showing off for Hannah and Rainy Day, who watched from outside the ring. I brought him to a halt and shivered.

All week the weather had stayed windy and chilly. Around the whole farm, leaves were drifting down from the old oaks and sycamores. The needled branches of the evergreens—the cedars, junipers, and firs—waved in the steady breeze. Behind me, Shawn wheeled up in what he called his ATC—his all-terrain chair.

"He's lookin' good," he said, meaning JP.

"Considering we don't get to work him every day, he's doing great," I said.

"When can you put a saddle on him anyway?"

"Not for ages. He's got to be at least one. So that's next summer, I guess."

Shawn took off his baseball cap, scratched his head, and put his cap back on.

"So what are you up to?" I asked.

"Same old, same old," he replied. "Helping Nelson out. Lots of reading at night. I'm a little sore from the twisting and extra movements of this work. All this reaching and throwing. Guess I'm just not used to it."

"Hey, Shawn," I said, suddenly struck with an idea.

"Yeah?"

"You want to go for a ride? On Rainy Day, I mean."

"Ha-ha, April."

"I'm not kidding," I said. "I'm doing this equine-assisted therapy. You know where kids with various conditions ride on horseback? I bet it would be great for you. And I'm an official volunteer now. I was screened last weekend. I know what I'm doing."

"Yeah, yeah, I think you mentioned this the other night at dinner."

"Right, well, how about it? I bet it would do you good. You'll be great. And Rainy Day's gentle and steady as a park bench."

Shawn looked over at Rainy Day. He paused just long enough to launch me into action.

"Let me just turn out JP and saddle Rainy Day. He and I have to ride home after we're done, so we can't spend more than twenty minutes or so anyway."

"I don't know, April…"

"I do. Come on. Wait here for just a second."

I unclipped JP from the long line and led him out to Hannah. Then I led Rainy Day into the barn, brushed him down, and put on all his new things. When we came back outside, Nelson was standing beside Shawn. That was good, because I thought I might need help getting Shawn up and into the saddle. I led Rainy Day into the ring and pulled the gate shut behind us. Then I remembered that my Willow Grove Stables volunteer ID was in the pocket of my sweatshirt. Just for a laugh, I got it out and clipped it onto my shirt.

"Oh, now that really makes me feel so much better," Shawn said sarcastically.

"I thought it would," I said.

Nelson put one foot up on the metal fence and playfully warned me to be careful.

"This is my employee you're experimenting with," he said. "Patti will probably kill me for letting you do this, but

I have confidence in you. And in Shawn's arm strength to hang on."

Shawn rolled his eyes but did not say anything.

"Okay," I said, having steadied Rainy Day along the fence and wound the reins around the saddle horn. "Shawn, get over on this side. Nelson, I need you."

It was a group effort, with Nelson basically shouldering Shawn up into the air until Shawn could use his own arms to pull himself into position. In a minute or two, Shawn was sitting tall in the saddle, his thin legs dangling loosely on either side of Rainy Day. I placed both his feet into the stirrups as he gathered the reins in his hands. Nelson stood back and whistled.

"Dude, you look awfully fierce up there," he said.

"Gracias," Shawn said. "Now what?"

"Now we'll move," I said. "I'll stay here by Rainy Day's head, and you stay put."

I took the reins from Shawn and passed them over Rainy Day's head so that I could control where we went. I repeated to Shawn all the things I had learned from Daniel.

"Just by sitting there, you're working muscles that people not in wheelchairs work by walking," I said.

"Huh?" Shawn's eyes were fixed on Rainy Day's mane.

"Try to relax a little more, Shawn. The horse's walk

works your abdomen. Also, you don't even realize it, but you're stretching your thighs and strengthening the muscles in your legs, too. Daniel and Emma have been telling me amazing stories about kids recovering from all kinds of disorders thanks to this."

"Yeah, well, remember, I don't have a disorder, April. My legs don't work on account of a homemade explosive some guy cooked up in his kitchen."

"I know, I know. Just sit tight and try to squeeze your legs into the sides of the saddle. Trust me."

"April, I *can't* squeeze my legs," Shawn said. "Best they can do is hang there."

"Sorry," I said, tucking the toes of his boots deeper into the stirrups.

We continued in circles around the ring, first clockwise and then counterclockwise. After the first few minutes of complaining, Shawn stopped talking and seemed to be concentrating on the physical challenge of staying centered. When we finished, Nelson had gone back to whatever he had been doing.

"I have to admit, that was pretty cool," Shawn said. "I felt sort of like a centaur—half-man half-beast."

I laughed. "Well, I'd better go get Nelson to help me get you off."

"Hang on, I think we can do this," Shawn said.

"No, I don't know about that," I said doubtfully.

"Yeah, let me just think for a minute. All I have to do is reach down and grab the top of the fence. If you just brace me at the waist, I think I can hang from the fence and then lower myself into my chair. Go bring the chair around to this side."

Rainy Day stood perfectly still while I rolled the ATC into place between Rainy Day and the fence. I wasn't entirely comfortable with this part, and wished Nelson hadn't disappeared. But I didn't want to go against Shawn, either. I tethered the reins to the fence post and stood where Shawn indicated. He leaned toward the top rail of the rusty red fence post, while I acted like a pier, bracing up his chest as he tipped down.

"So far, so good," he muttered. Shawn's cap fell off and blew under Rainy Day in a gust of wind.

"Now lead Rainy Day a little away so I can pull myself off and dangle from the fence into the chair," he said.

"I don't like this, Shawn," I said. "I'm afraid you'll fall."

"April," he said, his voice congested from being almost upside down. "Please, it's too late now to change plans."

I stepped away and led Rainy Day one small step away from the fence. Then I watched as Shawn's right leg slowly slid over the top of the saddle and then…he crashed down against the fence and plopped into the chair roughly, swearing at nobody in particular. One of his legs had gotten caught on the arm of the wheelchair.

"Shawn, I'm sorry," I said, picking up his baseball cap and passing it to him.

"It's not your fault," he said, lifting his leg up and over the arm and placing his foot onto the chrome support. "It wasn't the ride, it was the dismount."

"I guess we'll have to work on that," I said.

"Yes, let's," he added.

Nelson came running back from the direction of the house. "I'm sorry, you guys," he said. "I was expecting a call I had to take at five." He looked at Shawn, who was rubbing one side of his rib cage with one hand. "How did you manage to get down?"

"We managed, we managed," Shawn said. "As a matter of fact, we took great pains to manage."

Just then we heard the sound of footfalls and heavy breathing coming from the direction of the road.

"Lo and behold," Shawn said. "What have we here?"

"I think it's runners," I said.

The pack of middle-school cross-country runners was just now visible coming over the ridge. Right in the middle of the clump was Lowell, beet red in the cheeks as usual when he ran. He broke away to come over to me and Shawn. All the others kept going.

"Hey," he said, panting and jogging in place. "It was a long run today. I wondered if you guys would be here. I haven't seen you in a while, Shawn."

"You guys are three miles out of town," Nelson said. "That is a long run."

"It's like basic training," Shawn said. "Only without the artillery."

"That's what it feels like," Lowell said. "Well, I'd better catch up. See you, guys."

"Come back and visit me sometime," Nelson called after him as we said bye.

We watched him run off to join the others. I wondered what Shawn was thinking, seeing all those young, healthy boys with fully functioning legs.

Then he turned and looked up at me.

"When's my next lesson?"

Chapter

12

The next afternoon was a Friday, and Shawn and I met back at the ring and did exactly what we had done the day before to get Shawn in the saddle with Nelson's help. Only this time there was no crashing dismount.

"My stomach is incredibly sore," Shawn had said at the beginning of the session. "I feel like I've been doing sit-ups all night."

"I guess that's a good sign," I said, leading Rainy Day in slow circles.

"Can we go a little faster today?" he asked.

I nudged Rainy Day into a slightly quicker walk, but refused to let him break into a trot. That seemed to be asking for trouble. I checked out Shawn's posture and saw that he was letting his upper body move forward and back in time with the steady walking pace.

"You feel solid in the saddle?" I asked.

"Yup."

"Okay, then," I said, bringing Rainy Day to a halt. I threaded the reins back over his head and passed them to

Shawn. "Then go ahead and steer yourself. Keep the two reins together. Like this. You can even wrap them around one hand like this if it's easier. But let them rest in the center so he doesn't feel that you want to turn. The littlest pressure is enough to make him go where you want. The littlest tweak back will make him stop, right, Rainy Day?"

"Where will you be?"

"I'll stay by his head just in case, but you're the one with the reins. Got it?"

"More or less."

"And walking only. No trotting."

Shawn clucked Rainy Day forward. As we walked along, I didn't have any kind of goal for what I was doing with Shawn. All I knew is that for him, riding Rainy Day was a good thing. I had tried to explain this to Aunt Patti over dinner the night before, when I told her about Shawn's first ride.

"Everything I've seen at Willow Grove tells me that this equine-assisted therapy works in ways people can't really explain," I said. "I mean, yeah, it works muscles and all that," I said, sprinkling extra salt on my mashed potatoes. "But there's just something about being around horses—I mean, you should have seen how happy and alert this one kid seemed just to hear a horse pass gas. Or this other kid, just to listen to the snorts or smell their smell."

"And for Shawn?" Aunt Patti asked.

"I don't really know," I said honestly. "I don't think he does, either. Maybe it has something to do with being on the back of a big strong animal. Maybe he feels some of that strength coming into him."

Aunt Patti looked thoughtful as we finished dinner.

The rest of that week was routine, except that after school on a couple of days I watched my friends compete in their various sports—Lowell in a cross-country meet and Ruby in field hockey. It seemed like the whole middle school came out to cheer them on. Cross-country was challenging to cheer for, because you had to dash from point to point around this golf course as the runners covered the 3.2 miles of the event. You saw them run by, then cut off the loop and watched them pass at another point. Field hockey was a lot more spectator friendly, with kids, teachers, and parents chatting and laughing in the stands throughout the game. I have to admit that the whole team thing—the uniforms, cheering, and general celebration of every single success—made me feel envious. When he crossed the finish line, Lowell looked rather green and sick to his stomach, but just a few minutes later he seemed so proud of himself. I think he was happy to be seen as someone who had done something so hard.

That weekend I showed up at Willow Grove on Saturday psyched for another round of volunteering with Rainy Day. Emma seemed especially glad to see me.

"April, this is going to be a really busy day," she said, giving Rainy Day a pat as he stepped down the ramp of our trailer.

"How so?"

"Daniel got his dates mixed up and booked an extra couple of people by accident. I've got you down to work with Tony first thing this morning, if that's okay."

"Sure. That's fine." I waved good-bye to Aunt Patti as she drove off for the day, leaving the unhitched trailer behind. "What's Tony's condition?"

"Well, actually he's autistic," Emma said, watching me as if to see how I would respond as we walked Rainy Day to the ring.

"How severe?" I said.

"Well, not so bad that he can't sit in a saddle and have a good time, but too severe to sit in a mainstream classroom."

"How old is he?"

"Nine, I think," she said. "His dad has brought him every single week for almost a year now."

We stood outside the ring, watching a couple of lessons going on. Lester was hitched to his pony cart, and Warrior was making his slow way around the circle with a little girl who sat grinning upon his deeply swayed back. Close by the horses and clients, volunteers with big smiles escorted the processions. I scratched Rainy Day on his forehead and combed his bangs with my fingers. Then I smoothed his blanket where it had rumpled up during the ride over, probably when he had pressed up against the side of the trailer. When I looked back at the ring, one of the little riders had taken a hand off her handlebar and was waving at Emma. Emma waved back and called out, "Woo-hoo, Lydia! Way to go!"

Emma sounded like one of the field hockey moms after a goal.

"Okay, April," she said, turning at the sound of tires on gravel. "Here comes Tony."

She went over to a dusty blue sedan that pulled up and greeted the boy and his dad. Tony got out and walked with his head down straight toward the barn. I noticed that his arms barely moved as he walked. They seemed pinned to his sides. His dad ran to catch up. He caught Tony by the arm and redirected him back to where I stood with Rainy Day. Suddenly I felt nervous. Like with Matt, it was going to be hard to predict what Tony would do. His autism was obviously much more intense than Matt's condition. I wondered who the other two sidewalkers would be.

I knew Tony required a lot of attention because the sidewalkers turned out to be Tony's dad and Emma herself. They would be on either side of him, while I would lead Rainy Day. Eventually we got Tony into his helmet and up into the saddle.

"Okay, boy," I whispered to Rainy Day. "Be extra, extra steady. I'm right here next to you, so no matter what, you don't have anything to be worried about."

Rainy Day nuzzled me under the arm, then lifted his head up and away, assuring me that he was ready for anything. I gave him an extra pat down the front of his chest.

We entered the ring. Tony didn't say a word, but every time I looked back, his expression seemed happy. Sometimes he twisted around to watch Rainy Day's back legs move in the slow rhythm of the walk.

"Eyes ahead there, April," Emma said.

"Sorry."

I snuck a glance at the four or five other clients parading around the ring. One little girl was half-collapsed over her handlebar, but even she was smiling. She yelled hi to her mom, who was watching and waving from the side.

The few hours before lunch passed quickly. After Tony, I sidewalked for a boy who arrived on crutches, and for a girl who was wheeled over to Rainy Day in a big heavy wheelchair, one not at all as sleek and high-tech as Shawn's. While these kids rode, their parents stood at the side of the ring and cheered them on.

Around noon I unsaddled Rainy Day and turned him out to graze in the shade. I took the lunch I brought from home and sat down with Emma and the other volunteers at a picnic table. I unwrapped my sandwich and a big slice of tomato fell out from between the bread.

"That's some tomato," Emma said.

"These yellow ones are from our garden. They're actually famous, these Patti Helmbach tomatoes."

Emma laughed. I twisted off the lid of my root beer and took a long sip.

"Hey, Emma?" I began, when there was a break in the conversation. "Have you guys ever thought of putting together a horse show?"

"Hmm?"

"I mean, some kind of special event, with spectators and all? I bet these kids would love to do what they're doing for an audience."

"I don't know," she said. "This is therapy. They don't really do it for anyone else. Some might like it. But others…"

"That's what you think," I said. "I've been watching for a couple of weeks now and it sure does seem like for some of these kids, it's quote unquote real riding."

Emma shrugged. "I guess we can think about it."

The rest of that day and into the next school week, all I could think about was the idea of putting on a horse show. Maybe it was seeing how nice Rainy Day looked in all his new gear. Or maybe it was remembering how happy many of the clients looked on horseback and how proud they seemed when they were riding. At any rate, I just happened to be thinking about Tony, the autistic boy I had worked with over the weekend, when Matt came scrambling into study hall. My stomach did that flop inside it always did whenever he was around. His hair was disheveled, as usual, but his shirt was tucked in. One shoe was untied.

Matt's entrance broke the room's silence, and the teacher in charge glared in our direction. I mouthed sorry on his behalf, and the teacher looked back down at his own work as Matt took a seat next to me. He pulled out a couple of textbooks and a red spiral notebook with a dented and wrinkled cover. In full voice, as if he didn't realize we were supposed to whisper in study hall, he asked me a couple of questions about an English paper that was due—the first assignment of the year. Then he jotted a note. I watched him for a second, working up my nerve, then I put my pencil down and scootched my desk chair closer to his.

"Matt? I don't know what you've got going on after school," I whispered. "In general, I mean…"

Any other person might have jumped in at this point and said what they were up to, but by now I knew not to expect that kind of feedback. I went on in a low voice.

"Would you want to hang out sometime? Come over or anything?"

"Come over? Come over where?"

This conversation could not be any more awkward, I thought. But I took a deep breath and resolved to see it through.

"My house. Just to hang. Watch a movie or whatever." Then, for some ridiculous reason, I blurted in a stage whisper, "I have this horse. My own horse. He's pretty cool."

"I don't care for horses," Matt said. "Sorry."

I told myself not to take it personally, or at least not to take it like the total rejection it felt like, but still, his blunt response hurt. I returned to the problem on my desk, comparing the exterior angles of two different triangles.

In typical Matt fashion, two minutes later he said something completely unexpected.

"I would like to play Wizard with you if you're free at lunch."

"Sure," I said, smiling. "But you're going to have to remind me of the rules. I haven't played since fifth grade."

At lunch, Matt barely touched his sandwich, he was so intensely focused on dealing the cards and arranging his hand. A couple of girls and three boys walked by and smirked at us, one saying something pretty rude. I stared them down as they passed but didn't say anything.

"Ignore them—they're jerks," I said to Matt. I realized comforting him wasn't necessary. He no more heard them than I heard Aunt Patti telling me to get off the phone when I was deep in a conversation. Matt hadn't even heard me say that they were jerks.

"So go ahead and draw a card," he said. "Then play an Energy."

It took me a few turns to remember the Wizard lingo. Playing an Energy meant laying out these enabler cards that had pictures on them of lightning, solar rays, atoms in fission, or some other kind of energy. With enough enabler cards laid out, you could bring out your wizards, who would then do battle against your opponent's wizards. Different wizards had different abilities. They could zap, cast spells, or deal all kinds of damage to each other. This was the part I had trouble keeping track of. Mostly, I paused at the beginning of my turn. When he saw I had no idea what to do, Matt would cue me on my next play and suggest what he would do if he were in my place.

A couple more kids drifted by and made cracks, but eventually Ruby sat down to watch us. Lowell did, too, lowering his tray next to Matt. Monica had obviously given up on us and found another clique. For the rest of lunch, I was in heaven. After all the teaching and guiding I had been doing lately, it was nice being on the flip side. Whatever Matt told me to do, I did, no questions asked.

"Can I have winners?" Lowell said.

"Sure," I said.

Even though it was like Matt was playing against himself, he won quickly.

"Good game," I said.

"Thanks."

Without ever looking up, he gathered the cards for the round with Lowell. I wished that lunch period could have gone on all afternoon.

Chapter

I could tell something was wrong the minute I arrived at Willow Grove the following weekend. A couple of cars were parked at odd angles in the driveway, and three clients and their parents were sitting on benches, nowhere near the horses.

"What do you think going's on?" Aunt Patti said. "Where are Daniel and Emma?"

"I don't know. I'll go in and check. You can go on and leave, though."

"I can wait," Aunt Patti said. "I'm not going into the shop today anyway. Nelson needs some help with the last-minute arrangements. The goats arrive tomorrow."

"Tomorrow already?" I said, having forgotten all about that part of his back-to-the-farm plan. I pulled out my backpack and slammed the passenger door of our pickup. "Okay, then, I'll be back in a sec."

I met up with Emma, who was coming out of the barn wiping her eyes. When she saw me, she smiled sadly.

"It's Warrior," she said, before I could ask what was wrong.

"No!"

"We got here this morning and found him unsteady on his legs. He was breathing fast so we called up the vet right away."

"Oh, poor Warrior," I cried. "What's happening now?"

"We've known for a while it could be any time," Emma said. "It's been day to day for a month or two, you know. This may be it. A few minutes ago he stumbled to the ground and now he's just lying on his side."

Emma sniffed and blew her nose in a wadded white ball of tissue.

"Can I go see him?"

Emma paused. "I don't know. It's pretty upsetting, April."

I paused for a moment before answering. It was going to be a death scene. A death scene involving a horse. Not as scary or violent as the trailer accident on the highway, but still ... death is death. My whole experience at Willow Grove had been going so well, I didn't want to see something so sad. On the other hand, it was probably selfish to avoid something sad just because I didn't want to deal with it.

"I know," I finally said. "I can handle it."

Walking into the barn, I thought of the first time I had

seen Warrior, just a couple of weeks before. Daniel had mentioned how old and ill he was, but it hadn't sunk in that he could actually die. Even in the last two weeks, he had had clients ride on his saggy back. He had been part of the life of the stable and made the people around him feel better.

Now Warrior was lying in his stall, panting hard. Every so often he tried to lift his head to look down at his side, but he was too weak to hold it in that position for very long. He grunted and lay it back down, as if exasperated.

"He's such a nice horse," I said quietly, watching Daniel sponge the old horse's head with cool water. The vet looked on grimly, then pulled a long hypodermic needle out of an equipment bag.

Emma put her arm around my shoulders but didn't say anything. Warrior's expression, usually so placid, seemed frightened because of the way his eyes were bulging.

"So what happens now?" I asked.

"Well, he can't breathe. This is it. He has to be put down."

"Now? Today?" I said. "How?"

"This is the hard part of what we do," Emma said. "Warrior won't suffer at all."

"But April, as awful as this is, we still have clients waiting," Emma said, leading me out of the barn. "Get

Rainy Day out and come over when you can to help get things going, because we've got to make a couple of changes regarding who rides who."

"I will." A part of me wanted to watch what happened next in the barn. A part of me did not. I must have looked like a zombie walking toward our trailer.

Aunt Patti was looking at me with her you've-just-heard-scary-bad-news-are-you-going-to-be-okay expression on her face. She couldn't help it, I guess. For a long time, whenever something or someone died, even on TV or in a movie, I did start to melt down. Death always brought back memories of when my parents were killed. But maybe now I was becoming quote unquote more mature or whatever. Warrior's death made me feel sad, but more because he was a good horse who had led a long and useful life, and now he was about to be gone. If anything, now it was Aunt Patti who cried more at these moments.

Before driving away she gave me a long hard hug.

"I love you," she said. "You're amazing."

I laughed and hugged her back. "Oh, I don't know about that."

I backed Rainy Day down the trailer ramp and hitched him to the fence of the riding ring. Then I headed toward the barn.

"Hi, April," Daniel said, coming out in his long strides.

"Hey, Daniel," I said. "I'm so sorry about Warrior."

"Me too," he said.

Neither of us knew what else to say. After a few seconds of uncomfortable silence, we both turned at a loud monotone voice shouting my name.

"April! April!"

It was Tony, who was running over from his car in awkward, lunging steps.

"Hi, Tony," I said. "Ready to go for a ride?"

But Tony had a limited vocabulary and was also unsure about how to reply to questions. His mom had explained that when he was in doubt, he simply repeated himself.

"April!"

"Hello, April," Tony's mom said.

"Hi. You can go ahead and get his helmet on and get him ready. I'll see who he's going to ride and bring him out."

"That would be great," she said.

There were enough volunteers that morning to make sure that the rhythm of the lessons went more or less as usual even without Emma and Daniel participating outside with us. Tony had been on Rainy Day the week before, so we kept that match. After Tony, I sidewalked for a girl

149

named Sally, who had multiple sclerosis and rode the little pinto, and then with another girl named Megan, who had gotten a spinal injury from a car accident when she was four years old. She rode the old dapple-gray mare.

Over lunch, after we turned out the horses for their grazing break, we all sat around with our bag lunches at the wooden picnic table. Emma came out of the barn and joined us.

"It's over," she said. "Warrior's gone."

"Oh, Emma," said a volunteer.

"He had great care," another one said. "And he made people so happy."

"I know," Emma said. "That toothless old guy had really done it all. I've gotta go back in, but I wanted you guys to know."

We sat in silence for a while, and then someone raised the subject of therapy. One of the other volunteers said she thought one reason equine therapy worked was because it was exercise disguised as fun.

"They think they're doing something that makes them like so-called normal people, and they are, but they're also doing something good for them," said this volunteer, whose name was Susan. She was around my age or a little older.

"I know," I said, after taking a sip of ice water from my thermos. "That's why I think a horse show would be amazing. For so many of the kids, this has become a routine. Fun, but still a routine. A horse show would give them a big special goal to aim for. We could have ribbons, and music, and some of them could even be judges maybe."

"We could name it in honor of Warrior," Susan said excitedly.

"Yeah," I said, "like the Whispering Warrior Invitational."

After eating, I found Daniel in the barn, where he was hosing out Warrior's stall. He had shoveled out all the straw, which was sitting outside in a wheelbarrow. I leaned over the edge of the railing and watched the water splash up against the walls. The hard steady stream whooshing out of the black rubber hose pushed all the remaining dirt and cakes of mud out the door. Daniel was so focused on what he was doing that he didn't see me there until he turned to spray the floor under where I stood. When he turned off the water, I brought up the subject of a horse show.

"Yeah, Emma mentioned that the other night," he said, looping the hose back into circles and hanging it on a hook by the open stall door across from me.

"What do you think?" I asked. "Susan and I are thinking it could be the Whispering Warrior Invitational."

"I think you may have something there," Daniel said. "I just wonder about the events. A horse show can be sort of a fussy thing, and I don't want our kids to experience any pressure regarding looks, or style, or all that stuff you need to pay attention to when you ride English style. If we're gonna do it, and this is what I told Emma, it's got to be fun. The way this program is fun. It's got to be an extension of what they do already."

I thought about this and totally agreed. Daniel pulled a hammer out of his back pocket and started to pound at the head of a nail that was sticking out from a low spot on one of the walls.

"What kinds of things did you say Warrior used to do?" I asked. "I mean, in his heyday."

"All that rodeo stuff," Daniel said. "Barrel racing. Calf roping. You name it."

"Well, what about that? We don't do a show, we have games instead. Events. Parades. Whatever."

Still crouched and hammering, Daniel looked doubtful.

"The kids will still have all their sidewalkers and supporters. But there can be barrels to go around. And we can rope anything, a chair, or something. Some of the kids can do it on their own. The others will have people right there who can help them. And everyone gets ribbons." The ideas kept pouring out as I imagined the whole scene. "Maybe some kids could be the opening presenters or ribbon presenters. What about it?"

Daniel stood up and gently tapped the hammer into his left palm. "Well, I have to admit it would be something new. Why don't we see what Emma thinks? Go find her and fill her in before we get started with the afternoon people."

I dragged Susan with me to make the case for a rodeo/horse show/general fall celebration. We found Emma scrubbing caked mud off Lester's hooves. Our basic argument was: Why should only regular kids who play sports get all the glory and fans and prizes?

"We're thinking that everyone should be able to participate in a group activity," Susan said.

"I hear you," Emma said. "It's just something we've never done. We'd need permission from the parents. We'd need extra time from you guys and the other volunteers. We'd need supplies and whatnot." She ticked off each of these needs on her fingers, then opened her arms up as if there were so many more things we would need, her five fingers were not enough to count them all. "And right now, to tell you the truth, I don't feel up to thinking about it, April."

Little Lester bent one of his rear legs and pulled the hoof Emma had just cleaned right through the dusty gravel of the barnyard. She sighed. From a distance I heard Rainy Day neigh loudly, then hop sideways in the pasture. I wondered what he was up to. A couple of cars were pulling into the parking area. Pretty soon we would have to get back to work. It seemed time to strike a bargain.

"How about if Susan and I organize all the supplies and activities so you and Daniel don't have to worry about anything but picking a date, getting permission from parents, and making sure all the staff and volunteers are available?" I said. "And if you don't like anything at all about what we propose, we don't have to do it."

"Deal," Emma said. "The good thing about being in a new field like EAT, I mean equine-assisted therapy, is that you sort of get to make up the rules as you go along. I actually think this could be just the thing for the kids with the brains that work just fine but muscles that don't. Maybe you kids have picked up on something we haven't had time to notice. And the fact that the day would be named for Warrior makes me glad, too. Poor old guy. He was a good horse."

Emma was right. If I had learned anything about death by then, it was that nothing and no one ever dies without some kind of new experience following right away. What happened to my parents gave me a young aunt to grow up with, and a whole different childhood than I would have had. As horrible as the interstate accident was, the death of all those horses led to Rainy Day and me finding each other. Mr. McCann's passing put Nelson in our little world and gave Aunt Patti a boyfriend. And now, if all went well, the memory of Warrior would inspire a new tradition at Willow Grove. I can't say these thoughts were exactly comforting, but even I could see that death could mark beginnings as well as ends.

Chapter

That afternoon driving home from working at Willow Grove I told Aunt Patti about the plan.

"I get it," she said. "Kind of like a harvest or fall festival, but for riders. It sounds fun."

"I know. Emma and Daniel are into it, I think. And I can just picture how cool those kids will feel performing for an audience. Maybe not the autistic ones, but the others."

We got home and I led Rainy Day to the grooming place outside his barn. I tried to give him a full bath every Saturday night after our work at Willow Grove. First I removed all the gear item by item and switched his bridle for a halter, then clipped him to the rail. There he had a pail of fresh water to drink and some oats to snack on. Then I carried away the tack and put it away. Next I brought outside the brushes, rags, combs, buckets, towels, and shampoo—everything I needed to get Rainy Day clean and comfortable.

The late-afternoon sunshine was warm, and I settled into our routine. Brushing out the dust and dirt was the first step. As always, I fell into a kind of grooming trance, just enjoying the warmth that rose up off Rainy Day's coat, and the feel of his solid strength under my hands. I didn't hear Lowell approach until he was right behind me.

"Hey, April."

I must have seemed startled.

"Sorry," he said. "Didn't mean to scare you."

"That's okay. What are you up to?" I returned to what I was doing, while Lowell patted Rainy Day on the nose and under the chin.

"Just hanging," he said. "You just get back from work?"

"Mm-hmm. Steady there, boy," I said to Rainy Day. "I know you don't like when I pull burrs from your leg, but I have to do it." Rainy Day turned his head around to watch me yank at the tiny balls of prickles. He must have stepped right through a patch of them.

"So, what are you up to tonight?" Lowell said as I stuffed each burr into my back pocket to throw away later.

"Nothing, I don't think," I said distractedly.

"That's good, because I was just wondering..."

And there it was again. That tone. Not the old familiar we've-been-neighbors-forever tone. But the new, uncomfortable, unsure kind of voice. I looked around Rainy Day's leg to see if I could read Lowell's expression. He was

157

flushed and looking down, and suddenly I felt really sorry for him.

"You were wondering…?" I said.

Lowell stopped patting Rainy Day's neck. He put his hands in his pockets and came around to my side. "Okay, April," he said. "I'm tired of being scared. I'm tired of things being weird. I know this sounds ridiculous, given how long we've been friends and all, but I'm going to ask you anyway. Will you go out with me?"

Once the question was out in the air between us, Lowell looked down and used the toe of his sneaker to make little piles of leaves and stones on the ground. I busied myself with pulling dirt out of the nubs of the currycomb. When I was done with that, I started to aimlessly yank hair balls out of the grooming brush. My mouth had gone dry, and I felt myself swallowing over and over again.

Even though I had suspected something like this was going to happen, I was not at all prepared. I knew this was the same Lowell I had played with in the backyard, making up pretend games, using Chase when we needed a bad guy or an extra good guy. We were practically like brother and sister. Except for that stretch of time in seventh grade when Lowell was having problems with his parents, being rude to teachers, and shutting himself up in his room, I had always felt closer to him than I had ever felt to anyone except Aunt Patti. We had done some amazing things together the spring before during the floods. We had worked side by side all summer....

I looked at Lowell's long, wavy blond hair. He had nice skin that was always kind of rosy, except when he was running, when he turned bright red. He had nice grayish eyes. And we could talk about anything at all. Or nothing at all. Some of my favorite times we had spent just watching TV in total silence. No doubt about it, in my heart of hearts, I loved Lowell.

But was this the kind of love a person had for a boyfriend?

I yanked more hair out of the brush and let them fall to the ground.

I had to tell myself no, it was not. As if to press the point, a little voice piped in to remind me of how I felt whenever I was around Matt, which was definitely different.

Lowell was now tying a blade of grass into a knot. The seconds that ticked by were the most awkward I had ever lived through. Finally, just as I was about to say something, Lowell looked at me. From the way his face fell,

I could tell that he could tell what I was about to say even before I said it.

Somehow we got through the next few minutes, though what we said is still a blur. I mustered something about being grateful that he and I were such good friends, and that I liked him so much.

"But not in that way, I know, I know," Lowell said, somewhat bitterly.

"It's true," I said. "Can't we keep things the way they are?"

"I don't see that I have a choice about that, do I?"

Luckily, there was a horse between us, who at just that moment lifted his tail. A big tannish clump fell to the ground and the smell of manure spread between us. Neither of us could keep from laughing.

"Dang it, Rainy Day. Can't I even have any dignity in rejection?" Lowell said.

"Are you okay?" I asked.

"No," he said, half serious and half joking. "I'm not okay. I gotta go, April. I'll see you."

Aunt Patti and Nelson were going out to dinner that night with some old friends, so I stayed home alone, too tired to do anything or call anyone. I was upset about Lowell but knew there wasn't anything I could do to help him feel better. I hoped he got himself together enough to call another friend just so he wouldn't be alone.

The next day over breakfast Aunt Patti reminded me that this was the day the goats were to arrive, and did I want to be there for it.

"They got dropped off at the crack of dawn," she said. "I can hardly wait to see."

"For sure," I said. "I'll meet you there. After all that slow patient walking Rainy Day did at Willow Grove, I think it would do him good to get out and stretch his legs."

"Sounds good. I'm going to leave right away. Nelson's going to need all hands on deck. Shawn's coming, too."

"I'll get there as soon as I can," I said, hastily slurping up my cereal.

There was no sign of Lowell in his yard or around the house when I went out to saddle Rainy Day. Oh, well, if I didn't see a sign of him later, I'd go knock on his door and make him come out. I mounted and we set off, first at a walk to get out of the neighborhood, then at a trot as we headed up along the county road and into the country. For the first time that fall, I felt a nip of cold in the air that brushed against my face as I rode.

"This is probably much more comfortable for you, boy, no?"

Rainy Day's lively, energetic, and high-stepping trot told me he liked the temperature just fine.

I couldn't believe my eyes when we arrived at the McCann place. To think this had been the sleepy, run-down farm I had known back in the spring when Mr. McCann was still alive. Then weeds sprouted everywhere, choking out the lilies and irises, and splaying across the rotting fences. Doors leaned off their hinges, steps were missing on the front porch, and the splintered beams in the barn and other outbuildings invited all kinds of flying insects to make their nests deep in the crevices. And all the while, Mr. McCann would sit rocking and smoking on his front porch, paying no attention at all to the ramshackleness of his property. He'd make me fetch him a cup of coffee and a slice of cake, and tell me one story after the next about the old days.

Those days were clearly gone now. Thanks to Nelson's hard work and determination, the McCann property was spruced up and ready for a whole new kind of farming. All through the summer Lowell and I had helped him rebuild and repair the buildings, repaint, weed, plant new flowers and bushes, and maintain the animals. Since the end of

August, Nelson and Shawn had been working nonstop on readying a couple of large pastures and a separate outbuilding for the first group of dairy goats. Nelson had bought mature females, Aunt Patti said, so that he wouldn't have to wait before getting started with milk production. And now, as Rainy Day and I arrived, here they were, all seven of them crowding around Shawn in his wheelchair. Shawn sat among them distributing vitamin pellets and arranging a salt block. The short-eared goats were mixed colors—brown and white, black and white, and some with patches of all three colors. One of them wore a collar with a bell that bonged when she moved. I yelled hi and walked Rainy Day to the horse barn, where JP and Hannah stood looking out over the top of their door.

I dismounted and unsaddled Rainy Day, then led all three horses one by one out to the pasture that was going to be reserved for them. Nelson had explained that goats nibble the grass down to the ground, leaving practically nothing above the soil. "There are some countries, like Cuba for example, that use goats instead of lawn mowers," he had said. "You just lead them to the side of the road you want to mow, and let them get to work. Before too long the place will look as smooth and low as the green on a golf course."

Hannah and Rainy Day trotted off a distance away from the goats, who were bleating and bonging and in general changing the whole sound of the place. One had broken away from the group and was examining the bottom of the fence, as if to figure out a way through. Eventually she gave up and picked up a thin stick in her mouth and started to chew.

JP, on the other hand, couldn't take his eyes off the new arrivals. He scampered right up the edge of his fence and peered at the action. He let out a loud neigh, as if to signal his presence to them. He looked almost offended that they didn't seem the least bit interested in him. Hannah nickered, as if to remind JP that she was still there if he wanted company.

I unlatched the gate to the goat pen and walked straight toward Shawn. The heads of the goats came up to my hip, and except for one, they all had big swollen udders. One after another they bumped their heads against me, as if searching for something good to eat. One grabbed hold of the tiny flap on my back pocket.

"Hey, Shawn," I said. "This is wild."

"April," Shawn said from the middle of the sea of goats. "You wanna help?"

"If I can, sure."

"Go up to the indoor pen, then. Your aunt Patti and Nelson are trying to unpack all the stuff and organize the milking equipment. I'm okay here."

I leaned down and petted the rough, knobby, wiry heads.

"You must be a guy," I said to the one goat without an udder.

"Yeah, I'm calling that dude Atlas," Shawn said. "He's gonna have his own place to hang when it's not breeding season. Nelson was telling me how the bucks get so musky, their smell can get into the milk and make it taste too strong."

"Whoa," I said. "That sounds pretty intense."

"Yeah, you don't want the milk to be anything but sweet, which it is when the male's smell can't get into it."

The goats' eyes were a caramel color, their pupils vertical black slits. One by one, they continued to check me out. Every so often, and for no apparent reason, they butted each other gently. One actually acted as if she were going to climb up onto Shawn's lap.

"Is Nelson going to name every one of them?" I asked. "It seems like he should."

"I don't know. You can ask. But watch out for piles of small round black pellets," Shawn said. And when I looked up questioningly, he added, "Goat poop."

"Looks like that will be impossible to avoid around here from now on."

In the shelter, off at one side, Aunt Patti and Nelson were assembling the milking stand. It was a small wooden stage with a ramp at one end for the doe to climb up on, and a place at the other end to brace her head and let her eat her goat feed. There was a place to slide in the pail to catch the milk. The stand reminded me of those old-fashioned shoe stores Aunt Patti took me to when I was little. You climbed up with the new shoes on so the salesperson could reach your feet more easily.

"Hey, babe," Aunt Patti said. "Isn't this amazing?"

"Pretty cool," I said, looking around the airy, low-ceilinged barn. There were nice clean places covered with fresh straw for the goats to sleep and rest, a hayrack, a grain trough, a water pail filled with fresh water, and shelves for supplies and extra feed. A thin wall that went almost but not all the way to the ceiling would separate the does' area from the buck's. I could feel a light breeze coming through vents near the roofline.

"Yeah, in my dad's day, this old outbuilding was just a place he stashed equipment," Nelson said. "Or broken furniture he couldn't bear to part with. It's perfect for this.

Buster's already acting like he's got a new lease on life, as if he's some sort of goat guard or something. Every time one of them gets curious about the fence, he rushes over, barking to make them think twice."

"How can I help?" I asked, looking at the stack of bags of goat chow along one wall, and the scrubbers, pails, and washcloths, bottles of bleach, and other supplies.

"It would be great if you could set up the record-keeping system for me, April," Nelson said. "Like the one you do for JP? For each doe, we need to keep track of feed, milk production, medications, and breeding dates. I've got all the binders and paper, but nothing's organized."

I went over to the shelf that had all the supplies, and used my teeth to tear the plastic off the pad of ledger paper.

"For some reason when you said you were going to raise goats, I was expecting a lot more than seven," I said.

Aunt Patti and Nelson were done with the stand by now, and stood holding hands at the door of the shed, admiring the McCann place's new residents.

"Just wait till February," Nelson said.

"What happens then?" I asked as I opened the binder rings with a loud snap and loaded in the paper.

"Well, if everything goes according to plan, the buck will do his job with these gals this fall, and we'll have a batch of kids born five months later. That gives us five months to get up to speed with the milking routine."

I laid out the book with a page for each animal, which for now I numbered one through seven. I marked out columns for each of the categories Nelson had mentioned, as well as for the date.

"Shawn," Aunt Patti called out, "you sure look happy out there."

"Hey, this is the life," he replied, grinning. "I'm the center of attention for a half dozen intelligent females who have nothing better to do than hang around me."

"Why don't these goats have any ears?" I asked, getting up and joining them.

"They do, honey, they're just very small ones," Nelson said. "It's the breed. They're called LaManchas. I picked this kind because they're sweet, calm, and gentle compared to some of the others, who can be more feisty and stubborn. Plus I got a great deal on them from a local Missouri guy in Lebanon—a little more than a couple hundred dollars each, and he threw in a bunch of this equipment."

"Hey, Nelson," Shawn called. "You want me to clear away this brush pile along the east fencing?"

"No, thanks, Shawn. I put that there for the goats.

They need roughage every single day—twigs, branches, stalks."

"That's good to know," Aunt Patti said. "I'll bring over my dry cornstalks now that the growing season's over."

"Well, they're super cute," I said, "and I can hardly wait to learn how to milk, but now it's time for Shawn's riding lesson, remember? Remember, Shawn?" I called out more loudly.

"Maybe we should skip a day, April," Shawn said. "There's a lot going on over here."

"No, really, Shawn," Nelson said. "It's okay with me. We're fine until evening. Go ahead and ride."

Shawn shrugged and wheeled himself away from the goats and toward the opening in the fence. Two of the brown-and-white ones followed him.

"Getting in and out of here without letting them escape will be a challenge," he said to me, and I realized he was right. Even with both of us pushing their little heads back and making the gate open to as narrow a width as possible, it was touch and go. Thankfully, Buster came over and did his herding routine, nipping at the little hooves until the goats lost interest and turned back to the others.

"Good boy," I said to the old hound.

"Listen, April," Shawn said as we headed for the horse

barn, his ATV wheelchair bumping over the ridges of grass. "I don't feel like plodding along on Rainy Day. It's been fun and all, but if we're doing this, I'd rather go someplace. It's therapy whether I ride in circles or along a road, no? I would rather get out of the ring. And I would rather ride Hannah. She's bigger, and no offense, but she seems to have a little more life in her."

"Well, yeah," I said. "But I can count on Rainy Day to be steady no matter what. Hannah's not been ridden as much in general, and she wasn't screened for doing this the way he was."

"Hannah knows me," Shawn said dismissively, "and she's a solid old horse. Come on. It's not as though we're going out on patrol in an underarmored Hummer," he added, sarcastically referring to the circumstances of his getting wounded in Iraq. "We'll be fine."

It was against my better judgment, but I agreed. After all, Shawn was older than me, and I didn't feel right telling him what to do. So I saddled Hannah and led her up next to Rainy Day. I tied them both to the fence and wheeled over the contraption that Shawn and Nelson had constructed for Shawn's mounting and dismounting. I lined it up right next to Hannah, who certainly did look perfectly peaceful and calm. Shawn pumped himself up the ramp in his wheelchair, onto the landing that was nearly at saddle height. Then, using his incredible arm strength, he got himself into the saddle. It was an awkward move, but he did it completely on his own. I rolled our horse-boarding gizmo back to the barn door, shoved the wheelchair up against the fence, then came back and passed Shawn the reins. I mounted Rainy Day.

"Let's just make a couple of circles first, Shawn," I said. "Humor me. And if we go out on the road, we're not going to trot."

"Deal."

He clucked Hannah around so that she was walking along the outside of the ring while I followed, watching his movements and her responses. Out of the corner of my eye, I saw JP frolicking in a far corner of the pasture. I hoped his antics wouldn't distract her.

"Now let's turn and go clockwise," I said.

"Yes, ma'am."

I had to admit that Shawn's form looked really good. He sat tall in the saddle and held the reins centered, gently, and with confidence. He was a natural rider.

"Okay," I said, after we had completed our third circle. "Out we go." I slipped off Rainy Day and led him to the gate, which I swung open in order to let Shawn pass.

Out on the road, Hannah fell into step behind Rainy Day on the right-hand shoulder of the dirt road, which is how I wanted it. I knew I could trust Rainy Day not to break from the pace I allowed him. It meant that I couldn't watch Shawn, but I had to trust that he knew to take it easy. So as to avoid traffic if possible, we headed away from Plattsburgh. Since it was a Sunday morning, hardly anyone was out anyway. The road was nice and shady, and the horses seemed relaxed. The simple, two-beat rhythm of their slow walk meant that Shawn and I could carry on a conversation.

"So, are you still sore?" I asked.

"Not really," he said. "That went away after a few days. It reminded me of how agonizing all the physical therapy was when I first got back."

"I know what you mean," I said. "Lowell complained nonstop when he first started running."

"What's with Lowell anyway?" Shawn said. "I haven't seen him for a while."

I wasn't sure what to say, but knew that if I didn't say anything Shawn might assume something was wrong. All day, a part of me had been worried about Lowell since he had asked me out the night before.

"He's just really busy," I said. "He's got cross-country,

and the newspaper, and schoolwork."

Shawn said nothing, and I let the subject slide. We walked on in silence, each lost in our own thoughts.

What happened in the next few seconds is still hard for me to figure out, but I know I heard the break in Hannah's step as she stumbled on a loose stone. Then there was Shawn's swearing and a thumping sound, and when I looked around, he was pitched sideways out of the saddle and falling onto his side into the ditch. The saddle itself had slid off, which meant that the girth must have been too loose. Shawn was lying in an awkward heap, and Hannah was standing and blinking with the saddle hanging off her, looking patient as a cow.

Chapter

15

"Whoa, Rainy Day," I said, bringing him to a stop and jumping off. "Jeez. Oh, no. Shawn? Are you okay?"

"No, I'm not okay," he said, and I realized with a pang that this was exactly what Lowell had said, and that both of them were not okay on account of me. How could I have missed the correct hole when buckling Hannah's girth?

"Can you move?" I said, forcing back tears of guilt and fear.

"I'm pinning my own arm," he said, grimacing in pain and adding another round of curses. "Roll me over, April."

I looked at the two horses and trusted that they would stand still even if a car came by. I wedged one hand under Shawn's bottom arm to brace it and gently lifted and pushed until he was on his back with the limp arm folded across his chest. Sweat had broken out on his face as he stared up at the leaves waving over us.

"So now I'm down to one functioning limb out of four," he said, raising his good left arm and letting it fall to the ground. "Twenty-five percent working, seventy-five percent dead. And it's the hand I write with."

"Do you think it's broken?" I asked, swallowing hard to keep myself from crying.

"I have no idea," he said.

"Right now we've got to get you back and checked out. And we've got to get ourselves out of the road. This is all my fault," I blurted. "I knew this was a mistake."

"And that's why it's my fault," Shawn said. "I pressured you into doing this to show my beastliness. You wanted to stay in the ring, where I really belong."

Shawn's voice cracked, and then I really started to cry.

"Well, either way, we need to get you up now," I said, getting a grip. "There's no way you can ride back. Let's get you up off the road against that tree. Then I'll get the saddle back up on Hannah properly and ride Rainy Day back while leading Hannah. And I'll come back with either Nelson or Aunt Patti, and we'll get you to the ER. That's the plan. You're going to be fine."

As I dragged Shawn up out of the ditch from under his shoulders, he pushed and prodded his weight along with his left arm. Leaning back against a cedar tree bristling with peeling bark, he reminded me of the Scarecrow in *The Wizard of Oz* after the flying monkeys came and tore out all his stuffing.

"I'll be back as fast as I can," I said.

I led Hannah by the reins, walking beside Rainy Day. Steady old mare that she was, she followed obediently at the quick walking pace Rainy Day and I set. My hands were shaking, and I tried to grip the leather ever more tightly. Ever since getting Rainy Day, I had pushed aside the memories of my mother getting thrown. I knew that horses were powerful animals capable of harming or even killing a person by accident. But I had grown to believe that I knew enough to prevent anything terrible from happening. Shawn's fall felt like a blow to the entire world I had been creating for myself.

Back at Nelson's, I tied them both inside the paddock and sprinted into the main house, where I found Aunt Patti in the kitchen sterilizing the milking pails. The story came out in a rush, and was totally garbled because by now I was outright sobbing. Aunt Patti dropped the steel pail into the sink with a clang and followed me outside.

"Come on, then, April, get in the truck with me and let's go get him."

There were times when Aunt Patti could sense that I was being harder on myself than she could ever be, and this was one of those times. There was no "I told you so" lecture, no finger wagging or eye rolling. The only thing either one of us could think about was Shawn lying by the side of the road. Aunt Patti yelled into the main barn for Nelson, and the three of us climbed into our pickup and zoomed off.

Although it had seemed farther, Shawn and I must have ridden only about a half mile before he fell.

"That was fast," he said, grinning, even though his pale and sweaty face showed that he was in pain.

"Hey, buddy," Nelson said, bending over and gently laying the hurt arm across Shawn's stomach. "Patti, lower the tailgate, would you please? April, help me get Shawn up and into the truck bed."

Making a kind of seat with our arms, we got Shawn into the truck and stopped off at the farm for his wheelchair, which he requested. We sped off to the emergency room at the hospital in Union.

It turned out to be a clean break in his humerus—the bone in his upper arm. The doctor put him in a cast and told him it would take about four weeks to heal.

"So no riding for a while," he said, winking.

"Hey, no worries there," Shawn said. "I'm done with horses for good. I don't know what I was thinking."

Which made me feel awful. I almost wished Aunt Patti would have said something, or that Shawn would have yelled at me. And here I thought I was spreading the amazing influence of equine-assisted therapy!

Once Shawn had some painkiller in his system and knew that he would be fine in a matter of weeks, he was back to his jokey old self, even though I was not. On the way home, as we both sat in the back of the pickup truck, he teased me about the accident. With his good hand, he tugged one of my braids.

"Interesting therapy you got going there, April."

His words felt like needles, and when he saw that I felt genuinely horrible, he laid off the cracks. After a few minutes, he turned to me in all seriousness.

"No kidding, April, when I'm healed, I want to try riding again."

"Really?"

"Yeah. That centaur feeling blew my mind. I find myself dreaming about it at night. But, no offense, I think from now on I'd like to do it at that place you work."

"Willow Grove?" I asked.

"I guess. Sometimes you gotta do things by the book. I know you meant well, but . . . "

"I know, I know," I said.

We dropped Shawn off at his apartment, where his mom met us to let him in and watch over him the rest of that day and evening.

By now it was lunchtime, and we went back to Nelson's. Hannah and Rainy Day had been standing around in their saddles since we had left for the hospital, and they looked at me expectantly. JP had drifted over to Hannah, as if wondering why she and Rainy Day were not budging. He kept snorting and nickering. The other animals were simply going about their day. Over in the barnyard, Old Moses, the pig, snooped along the feeding trough for scraps. A small group of black-and-white chickens pecked at the bits of grain spilled under the overhanging eave of the barn. And the little herd of goats had their heads down in the grass of their yard, tearing up the blades and grinding their jaws from side to side.

"I'm sorry, you guys," I said to Hannah and Rainy Day. "I know you want to get out in the grass."

I removed all the tack and turned them out. JP galloped ahead, racing them out to the green fields. After hanging up the saddle, the saddle pads, and the bridles, I trudged across the barnyard, up the main house porch steps, and into the kitchen. I went straight to the sink to wash my hands.

"So," Aunt Patti said, ladling a portion of a thick orange-colored soup into a bowl and passing it to me.

"There's bread and cheese on the table. Nelson's just washing up."

"Smells good," I said. "What is it?"

"Butternut squash."

"From our garden?"

"You bet," she said.

Nelson came in and we all sat down to eat. All the things that might have been said hung in the air unsaid. After lunch, I cleared my bowl.

"Since Shawn's not here," I said to Nelson, "how about I clean Hannah and JP's stall before heading home? Is there anything else you need me to do?"

"I think that's it," Nelson said.

"Then I'll do that and then take off. I think I'm getting together with Ruby tonight, if that's okay. Her mom's dropping her off after dinner sometime."

"Sounds like a plan," Aunt Patti said. "I'm going to spend the rest of the day here and help with the first milking."

At home later that afternoon, I lingered over Rainy Day's grooming and thought about everything that had been happening in the last few days and weeks. The things and also the people—Tony and the other kids at Willow Grove, Matt, Lowell, and now Shawn. While currying around the white patch in the middle of his forehead, I caught a glimpse of Rainy Day's glossy brown eye looking straight at me. I patted the velvety smooth spot above his lip, and the hard mounded surface of his strong jaw. I was beginning to think certain ideas that might seem good at first turn out to be really very bad.

The next weekend started off gray and looking like rain. On the way over to Willow Grove, Aunt Patti was exuberant about the goats.

"And you should see how creamy the milk is, April. I read someplace that the fat in goat milk doesn't separate as easily as cow's milk does, so it's naturally creamier. And so white. And they're just so cute standing there eating away on their stand while you milk them. At first it was hard, but eventually I got the hang of it. We did all six in about an hour. Nelson says it'll get faster as we get better. I can't wait for you to give it a try."

I was staring straight ahead but I could tell she snuck a glance at me.

"April, babe, you've got to stop beating yourself up about what happened to Shawn. It was an accident. You can take responsibility and feel sorry up to a point, and I am glad to see you do that, but after that you have got to let it go. Everyone else is going to."

"I can't, Aunt Patti. And it's not just that. It's other things, too."

"Like what?"

"Oh, just stuff. I'd rather not talk about it right now."

Deep down, I knew that Shawn and I would eventually get back to the teasing way we had been before his fall. Now I was thinking about Lowell, and Matt, and the different ways these friendships kept changing. What happened when one of the people wanted things to be different? How much should a friend try to make things change? Should I be making more of an effort to like Lowell the way he liked me? How long should I go on letting myself like Matt when it was clear there were pretty severe limits to the ways he could be friends with anyone, let alone more than friends with me?

We pulled into the gravel circle at Willow Grove and got Rainy Day out of the trailer. As usual, we unhitched it so that Aunt Patti could drive around without it all day while I worked. She gave me a tight hug good-bye.

"See you later, babe. Remember, ease up."

"I'll try, I guess," I said.

Because we had been running a little late, Tony was

already waving hi from the main entrance, where he stood with his mom and Daniel. Tiny flying insects swirled around the barn door, the ones that always did when it got gray and seemed like it was about to rain. Tony didn't seem to mind them, but I saw him mom swat back and forth with her free hand.

"Hi, Tony!" I said. "How are you today?"

"April!" he said. "Rainy Day!"

Daniel fastened on his helmet and hoisted him into the saddle. He beckoned over another sidewalker volunteer, who stood on one side while his mom stood on the other. We entered the ring and began making slow circles. I could hear Tony laughing and giggling and yelling as we moved at a snail's pace.

After Tony's time was up, Rainy Day and I gave a ride to Megan and Claire, both little girls, and both of whom had spinal problems that made walking impossible. Every so often I turned back to face them and saw their faces beaming with pride as they sat in the saddle.

The morning lessons were over just as the sky opened up and it began to rain. We led the horses under the unwalled shelter where they would stay dry, and all of us volunteers, plus Daniel and Emma, hurried into the open area of the barn with our sack lunches. I asked Daniel and

Emma if I could sit with them, and they slid over to make room for me.

"I've been thinking about that whole Warrior Invitational idea," I said.

Daniel nodded while taking a huge bite out of a tuna salad sandwich.

"I don't think it's such a good idea anymore." Daniel and Emma both raised their eyebrows. I was prepared for that.

"These guys really all do seem perfectly content and proud the way things are," I said. "What they're doing isn't a show, and they don't need the hoopla and excitement of a show. They're just pleased—more than pleased—to come here and do what they can count on. Ride around on nice gentle horses for their own pleasure. It helps them physically, of course, but I've been watching them, and mostly it helps them feel good in the moment."

"I hear what you're saying, April," Emma said. "And I think you're right."

"Me too," said Daniel.

"I just feel like, who am I to come here and butt into what's already working perfectly fine and change it? There are things you try to change and things you should leave alone, I guess is what I've been thinking."

What I did not say, but could not stop thinking, was that it took a major accident for me to realize that I ought to have left Shawn alone. Not everyone needs to find happiness on the back of a horse.

Chapter

16

"You sure seem like you're in a better mood now than when I dropped you off," Aunt Patti said as I jumped into the passenger seat next to her and slammed the door. I was humming a song that had been stuck in my head all afternoon, reaching for the high notes and laughing when they came out flat and wrong.

"I am," I said. "Let's get home, though. I've got loads of homework for tomorrow that I haven't touched."

"That's too bad," Aunt Patti said, slowly veering out of the gravel driveway and turning onto the road back to Plattsburgh.

"Why too bad?"

"Because I was hoping you could come over and learn how to milk the goats. It's so cool."

"I just can't tonight. I'm sorry. Maybe if I get done."

"See what you can do. It's only three now."

Aunt Patti turned on the radio and we drove the rest of the way singing along to top 40 songs. On our street she slowed down to make the turn, and I noticed a figure sitting cross-legged on our front porch.

"Now who's that?" Aunt Patti said, squinting behind her glasses.

"I don't know," I said. "Wait, I do know. It's Matt."

"Matt? The new boy you've been talking about? The one Nelson thinks has—"

"Yeah," I said, waving to him as we slowly rolled into the driveway and toward the garage. As soon as Aunt Patti stopped the car, I jumped out and ran back to the front of the house. I was covered with dirt, dust, and flecks of leaves from sidewalking at Willow Grove all day, and I smelled like a barn, but I knew Matt probably wouldn't notice any of that.

"Hi, Matt," I said. I tried not to sound totally surprised to see him sitting on my front porch for no apparent reason. A bike that must have been his was leaning against the little dogwood on our front lawn.

"Hello, April," he said, standing up. "You once said to come by sometime so I could see your horse and play Wizard again, so I rode my bicycle over."

"Wow," I said.

Just then Aunt Patti joined us, and I introduced them.

"Matt is interested in meeting Rainy Day," I said, trying to act like it was the most normal thing in the world.

"Great!" Aunt Patti said, and I was relieved that she was her most laid-back, relaxed self. "Nice to meet you, Matt. Can I get you anything to drink or eat? April usually comes back from Willow Grove starving."

"What's Willow Grove?" Matt said.

"It's just this place where kids with various—" I stumbled over how to phrase the description. "This place where various kinds of kids come to horseback ride. I help out there part-time. It's my phys-ed credit, actually."

"Oh, I see," Matt said, and I could tell he was filing this information away someplace where he could get it if he ever needed it again.

"Well, I'll just go in and make something light," Aunt Patti said. "April, I'm assuming you're going to get Rainy Day out and groom him before homework?"

"Yeah, okay, thanks. Matt, come on around here."

He followed me and watched as I unlatched the back of the trailer, opened the door, and slid down the ramp.

"This part can be a little tricky," I said. "Maybe you ought to stand back a little farther. He's got to come down backwards and very slowly."

Even after he moved, I still wasn't comfortable with where Matt was standing. "I mean, maybe off to the side, like here," I said, pointing to an exact spot. This time, when

I was specific about the instructions, he was fine.

I slipped into the narrow space between Rainy Day and the side of the trailer.

"Hi, boy," I whispered, patting his face and gathering the lead rope. I tucked myself up against his neck and shoulder and, watching where he placed each hoof, clucked him into motion. Rainy Day backed down the ramp and stood in the driveway looking at Matt, who was looking at him with wide eyes.

"So this is Rainy Day," I said. "You can pat his nose or neck or anything."

"Hello," Matt said, as if he were talking to a person.

Rainy Day pricked his ears forward, swung his head to the side, then dipped it down, as if he were communicating with another horse. I laughed and patted him.

"You want to come with me into the barn?"

"Sure," Matt said.

Looking at him and feeling the way I felt when I was around him, there's just no other way of putting it except to say that at that moment I would have given anything for Matt to be like a regular guy, a guy I could talk to and go out with like a regular couple. On the other hand, as we walked into the barn, a so-called normal guy would not have simply appeared on my front porch out of the blue.

He wouldn't be Matt without being this very Matt.

And this very Matt was hitting it off with Rainy Day. At his request, I handed him the currycomb, and he began passing it over Rainy Day's back and sides as if he had been grooming horses all his life. The look of concentration on Matt's face as he cleaned out the grime was amazing. While Matt worked, I hung up and stored all the riding equipment. We worked side by side in complete silence, but it wasn't at all awkward. Actually, having watched the more severely autistic kids at Willow Grove, I recognized the look of pure satisfaction on Matt's face. Rainy Day stood stock-still for him, every so often stepping down hard with one hoof to rid himself of a fly or just call attention to that leg. Once he craned his head around to check exactly who this person was who was grooming him with such care.

Outside, the wind picked up again, and I could hear dry leaves blowing in the street behind the barn, which sat on the back edge of our property. A shutter banged open against the side of the barn, startling a swallow up and out of his nest. He swooped outside as if to check the weather conditions, then came back in. I filled Rainy Day's feed bucket with a mixture of oats and grain, and hung it in front so he could eat while Matt, now using the soft brush, worked down each one of Rainy Day's legs.

"That looks good, Matt," I said, when it seemed like he would have kept going all the rest of the afternoon. "You're done."

He put the tools down and stood back to watch Rainy Day eat. He looked closely at Rainy Day's flexible lips grabbing at the feed and listened to the loud hollow sound of the grinding teeth. He stood mesmerized for several minutes while I wondered if we ought to make a dash for the main house before the rain came. Outside, a crack of thunder told me we had to make a move.

"Do you want to play Wizard?" he said.

"Sure. You want to go inside, though?" I asked, indicating the kitchen window we could see from the barn. Because the sky was darkening with clouds, Aunt Patti had turned on the light. And she was right. I was pretty hungry.

"How about in here?" he said.

"I guess we could stay here," I said doubtfully. I was afraid if I insisted on going back to the house, Matt might make one of his unpredictable dashes to his bike and disappear, even in the rain. And that I definitely did *not* want to happen.

So, even though it's hard to believe, that's how Matt Heisman and I came to be seated on the floor of the barn by my desk on top of a saddle blanket in a rainstorm playing Wizard on a random Sunday afternoon. During a break in the downpour, Aunt Patti brought out a tray of lemonade, chips, and guacamole, which we ate while we played round after round of a game that captured and held Matt's attention like a magnet.

In the course of that afternoon, I realized that what I felt for Matt, Matt would never feel for me. To him, I was simply another person. I was a person he could do things with, and even enjoy being around, but he would never get whatever you want to call it—romantic—with me. And maybe not with anyone else. I sighed a couple of times as I ordered the different levels of wizard cards in my hand. Some were powerful, some were weak. But like in any game, no matter what I might have hoped for, I was dealt those cards and no other ones.

Sometimes all you can do is hope you have the energy card that will enable your best wizard.

It could have been that an hour or two went by before Aunt Patti came rushing back out to the barn with her purple poncho on.

"Matt's mom's on the phone," she said to me. "She wants him to come home as soon as the rain lets up."

"All right," Matt said. He had not shifted from his cross-legged position, which I had noticed because his hip joints were so loose that his knees lay flat on the blanket. He gathered up the cards, toted up all our points, and declared that he had won by something like ten thousand years' worth of spell credits.

"We have an hour or so before dinner, April," Aunt Patti said before turning away. "I'm just going to run over to Nelson's while the casserole bakes. I know you've got work to do."

"Homework," I said to Matt, who nodded as he threaded the well-worn rubber bands around each of the Wizard decks.

"Matt? We could throw your bike in our truck and give you a ride home. In fact, I think we should. Call your mom back, why don't you?"

Matt got up and spent a few minutes patting Rainy Day around his head and neck. He brushed the back of his fingers against the soft part of Rainy Day's nose and even leaned his cheek against Rainy Day's. It reminded me of what Daniel had said about how for kids like Matt, all the senses were stimulated by caring for animals, without the complicated feelings of people and social expectations getting in the way. When he was interacting with Rainy

Day, Matt seemed so much more natural than when he communicated with humans.

For those few seconds, but only for those seconds, I wished I were a horse.

Chapter

Warm and wiry goat hair shifted into my forehead as I leaned forward and tried for the fifth time to get decent grips with both hands on the teat of the fawn-colored doe I had decided to call Falstavia, which was one of the characters in Wizard. Falstavia stood on the milking stand, nibbling goat chow out of a pail, fairly patiently considering all the tugging and yanking I was doing.

"It's not straight down," Nelson said, encouraging me to keep trying. "It's more a slow, gentle but firm pull that starts at one end of your hand and works its way down. You'll know it's right if you get a long steady squirt into the bucket."

It was a few days into the following week when I finally got around to learning how to milk a goat. Aunt Patti and I were going to have dinner with Nelson, so she and I came over when she was done at Room for Blooms.

"Try turning your head to the side so your cheek is lying against her instead of your forehead," Nelson said.

Falstavia gave a small bleat, as if to suggest that this

might not be a bad idea.

Squeeze. Pull. Squeeze. Pull. Pull. Squeeze.

Chhshshshshshshwwwwwwwt!

A long hard stream of warm milk came down onto the sides of the pail with enough pressure to splash up into my lap.

"I did it!" I cried.

"Nice job, April," Nelson said. "But you gotta keep going. One side after another, back and forth. Now that you've got the angle, keep it up."

"For how long?" I asked, listening and feeling for that satisfying sound.

"Well, I'm at the point where I can empty a doe in about seven or eight minutes," Nelson said, standing behind me and looking over my shoulder. "I can do the whole lot of them in about forty minutes, when I get going. But I doubt you'll work that efficiently right off the bat. Just listen and feel. You'll know she's empty when nothing more comes out. It'll be about a couple of quarts or so, maybe a little more."

Behind me I heard Aunt Patti come into the shed.

"Where do you want these, Nel?" she said.

"Over there by the hayrack," Nelson said.

"Look at you," Aunt Patti said to me. "Way to go, babe.

Oh, Nelson, I hope it's okay—I invited Fran and Lowell over for supper. Walt's away in Jeff City for the night, and she had to work late."

I was glad I had my head against the side of a goat when I heard that little piece of news. Lowell and I had been avoiding each other ever since the awkward encounter a couple of weekends before. I was sure that he had even deliberately gone back inside his house for no reason. One morning he had come out, seen me, then acted as if he had forgotten something so he wouldn't have to walk with me.

"That's fine," Nelson said. "Shawn's around here someplace, too, so we'll have the whole workforce on hand."

At least there would be enough people around to dilute the tension, I thought, pulling steadily at the teats one after the other. Luckily, Aunt Patti was more focused on what they could serve for dinner than the effect of the guest list on me.

"I brought over a huge vegetable stew," she said, "the last of the eggplant, a bunch of tomatoes, onions, garlic, and various herbs. So I guess I'll go in and start some rice and then come back out to get this milk into the cooling pans and stored."

"Okay," Nelson said. "Come out when you can."

"There," I said, backing away from Falstavia's flank. "She's all done. Who's next?"

Just for fun, I had named a few of the other goats after Wizard characters.

"Saint Evangelina?" I called. "How about you go next? You or Shiva."

Before leading Falstavia away, Nelson came over and made sure every last drop had been milked.

"You really want to make sure there's nothing left. Any residual milk can cause an infection," he said.

I got through the rest of the goats and helped Nelson transfer the milk into cooling bottles. From the cold-water baths, the bottles would go into the fridge. He had moved the old basement refrigerator once stocked with orange soda into the milking shed.

Leaving the shed, I headed over to the pasture and Rainy Day came trotting over, expecting an alfalfa cube or some other treat. But my hands and arms were completely sticky with goat milk. He sniffed at me and I could have sworn he had a puzzled expression in his eye.

"Yeah, boy, I know it's a little weird, new species and all. You can take this, though," I said, passing him a sugar cube I had swiped from the cafeteria that afternoon. "I think I might let you have a sleepover tonight," I said. "You can stay with Hannah and JP, since it'll be dark after dinner. I hadn't thought of that."

Rainy Day swished his tail and turned away. Watching him move so freely around the McCann pasture, I was grateful that he had a farm to visit where he could really move around in a larger space. There was so much to do and see—the other horses, the other animals, more action and stimulation in every way.

By the time Miz Fran and Lowell arrived, the rest of us were in the kitchen, including Shawn, who was entertaining Aunt Patti and Lowell with a story about the time his tough-as-nails sergeant fell in love with a stray kitten.

"He wouldn't let anybody come near that cat," Shawn said. "She slept in his helmet." With his right arm, the one in the hard cast, he pretended to cradle an imaginary cat.

"Amazing," Nelson said.

"Hey, Lowell," I said, as tonelessly as I could manage. Actually, I was glad to see him.

"Hey."

"Fran, let me get you a drink?" Nelson said.

"Oh, anything's fine," she said. "Water, soda, whatever."

"Dinner should be in just a second," Aunt Patti said. "April, why don't you go show Lowell the goats? He hasn't seen them yet, and he's the one who started off the summer getting all that fencing cleaned up and ready to go."

Lowell and I looked at each other and he gestured toward the back door, as if to say, *Lead the way. I'll follow.*

We made our way to the goat shed without a word passing between us. But once we were standing among the seven does. Lowell broke the silence.

"Jeez, April," he said. "Look at this."

Lili and Carmen came over to check out Lowell's pockets, one intelligent little head nosed into each side and bleating.

"And what exactly are Nelson and Patti up to with this?" he asked, taking a step backward to dislodge himself from the prying does.

"They're selling the milk to organic grocery stores in St. Louis. And I think once they get the hang of that, they're going to make and sell cheese, too."

I went over to pet Falstavia, the pale reddish brown one. She would always be my favorite since she was the one I learned to milk first.

"So, when's that horse show thing you're organizing," he said, obviously trying to make a normal conversation.

"Oh, that. That's not going to happen. I guess I haven't seen you, or I would have mentioned why."

We both plopped down on the soft dry hay. Lowell took a stalk of hay in his hands and tried to split it down the middle. I picked one up and bent it into a loose knot. Then I took another one and made a sharply angled bow. A couple of the goats lay down in the hay not too far from us.

"I'm sorry for hurting your feelings, Lowell," I said. "I am, and I don't really know what else to say."

"I'm the jerk," he said. "I like things the way they are, too. I always have. It just sort of seemed like maybe we should make more of what we have. I mean, all the guys were saying, 'Go for it. You like her. Ask her out.' So I did. But I didn't really consider how that would change things between us. I don't know...."

I nodded because I think I understood exactly what Lowell was saying. Why is it that people generally wish for more when enough is just right? We must be wired that way, I guess.

Once we had cleared the air, it didn't take long for Lowell and me to find our way back to normal. We were too much like sister and brother. And siblings, at least the ones I knew, couldn't stay mad at each other for long. I took some time to explain what had happened to Shawn's arm, and my part in the accident. And how that was connected to backing out of doing a show or rodeo day at Willow Grove.

Aunt Patti called us into dinner and we got up. All of us sat around the big dining room table, the one that had belonged to old Mr. McCann. Aunt Patti and Nelson sat at either end, Shawn and Lowell sat on one side, and Lowell's mom, Miz Fran, and I sat on the other. Aunt Patti had lit candles and the piping-hot stew smelled like fresh herbs, just like fall is supposed to smell. A wooden bowl was heaped with emerald green lettuce and bright red radishes that glistened in the salad dressing.

Nelson raised his glass and Aunt Patti tapped a knife against hers until we stopped passing dishes around and got quiet.

"Welcome, everyone," he said. "I had planned to make an announcement at this dinner, but Patti changed my mind." He winked across the table at her, and she beamed at him.

Somehow I suspected that Nelson's announcement did not have to do with goats. If the news was what I was thinking, my guess was that Aunt Patti wanted to speak with me alone first. I scrutinized her face for clues, but her expression, although content, gave nothing away. Across the table from each other, Lowell and I caught each other's eye. He raised his eyebrows.

Questions bubbled up in my head. Did I want Aunt Patti and Nelson to get married? And if they did, did I want to move here, to the McCann place? If we did, Rainy Day would be happy, that much I knew. No more lonely days in our backyard while I was at school. He would have Hannah and JP to play with. Chase would have Buster. And I...what would I have?

Looking at each person sitting around the table, I realized that in every way that mattered, this was my family, and I could definitely deal with whatever came next. If trust meant letting go of doubt, at least temporarily, I was ready to trust life to run its course.

Nelson cleared his throat in mock seriousness.

"Friends, family, and fellow citizens," he began in a lofty style, "we are gathered together to feast. But before we do so, let us remember that everything we eat ultimately depends on the soil of the earth and the light of the sun. Let us be grateful for both light and dirt."

"You said it," Shawn joked.

"Here's to you all," Nelson said, raising his glass.

It hit me that I was starving, and I dug into the meal.

After dinner I helped clear the table, grabbed a few raw scraps, and then went out to the barn. Hannah and JP were settled down in their stall. Rainy Day perked up when he saw me approach. He came over, curious whether I had anything for him to eat. As it happened, I had a chunk of carrot in the palm of my hand. Rainy Day lipped it right out, and I listened to the sound of his teeth crunching. A year ago, who would ever have thought I would seek comfort in a barn?

But this really is me, April Helmbach. Daughter of Mary Beth and Harry Helmbach. A horse person out of thin air.

Glossary

bay—a reddish brown color used to describe horses

bridle—the entire headpiece, including the bit, chinstrap, reins, and headstall

canter—one of a horse's four basic gaits, a three-beat gait

cantle—the rear part of a saddle

colt—a male horse under four years old that has not been castrated

croup—the rump, or back part, of the horse

currycomb—a plastic or rubber comb with several rows of short flexible bristles used for grooming

dapple-gray—gray with a mottled pattern of darker gray markings

dock—the solid part of the animal's tail, not the hair

fetlock—the tufted, cushionlike projection on the back side of the leg above the horse's hoof

filly—a young female horse less than three or four years old

foal—a male or female horse less than one year old and still drinking their mother's milk

gallop—the fastest gait a horse can run

gelding—a male horse who cannot reproduce (unlike a stallion)

girth—a band or strap around the body of a horse that secures the saddle

halter—a harness of leather or rope that fits over a horse's head and is used for leading a horse

hock—the joint in the horse's hind legs similar to the human ankle

hoof pick—a metal or strong plastic tool with a pointed end for picking debris out of the underside of the hooves

mare—a female horse over four years old

Morgan—the oldest breed of horse originating in the United States, descended from a strong, fast, gentle, intelligient, and patient horse belonging to a Vermont schoolmaster named Justin Morgan in 1789

nicker—a sound a horse makes, presumably to communicate a greeting

paddock—an outdoor enclosure where horses are turned out for grazing

pastern—part of the leg between the hoof and the fetlock

pinto—a pattern of horse coloring characterized by two colors in particular patterns

poll—the topmost part of the head of the horse

rear—to rise up onto the hind legs

roan—a horse hair color characterized by a gray or white thickly interspersed with other colors such as bay, chestnut, brown, or gray

stallion—a male horse who can reproduce (unlike a gelding)

stifle—the joint in the horse's leg similar to a human knee

tack—all gear and equipment that can be worn by a horse, including the bridle, saddle, bit, and halter

Thoroughbred—a breed of horse used as a racehorse and for hunting and jumping

trot—a two-beat gait, with the legs moving together diagonally

walk—one of the four basic gaits, a four-beat movement where each leg moves independently and each hoof strikes the ground separately

withers—the slight ridge on the back of the horse

whinny—a low neighing sound